DEADEYE

DEADEYE
WE ARE FUCKED.

A NOVEL BY
BLACK PATRICK

BPP
BLACK PATRICK
PUBLISHING
LOS ANGELES

This magnificent book you are cradling in your hands is a work of fiction and a work of art. Any similarities to people sharing the same name as you appear within these pages because the author has a sick sense of humor. He or she may have suffered a stroke or two. Be grateful you may or may not be somewhat interesting to someone somewhere.

Stay calm. Don't be alarmed. It's just another day back at the funny farm. Don't fuck with me.

Copyright © 2024 by Black Patrick

All rights reserved. No part of this book may be used or reproduced in any manner whatsoever without permission except in the case of brief quotations embodied in critical articles and reviews.

blackpatrick.com

ISBN 9798330267569

3 5 7 9 10 8 6 4 2 1

Printed in the United States of America.

Published 2024
First edition published 2024.

BPP
BLACK PATRICK
PUBLISHING
LOS ANGELES

"What would Godzilla do?"
—*Black Patrick*

CONTENTS

SOMETIMES — 1
1. Nothing is not Easy — 3
2. Truck Stoppers — 9
3. Magic Bass — 13
4. Avocado Seed Squirrel Situation — 17
5. Train Train U.S. Tour — 21
6. Six Six Six U.S. Tour — 25
7. Fisting the F.B.I. — 29
8. Yacht Rock — 33
9. New Band — 37
10. East Coast Tour — 49
11. Jamaica — 51
12. Fire Tornado Records — 59
13. Solid Lineup — 63
14. Welcome to West Hurley — 67
15. Montreal — 71
16. Road Trip/U.S. Tour — 81
17. Nashville — 89
18. Los Angeles — 97

LIGHTNING STRIKES — 105
19. Back in Nashville — 107
20. New Orleans/U.S. Tour — 111
21. London Calling — 117
22. Wedding — 123
23. Movie Star — 131
24. More is Better — 135

25 Europa	141
26 Sverige	149
27 Shake it Up	169
28 Space Jams	173
29 Germany	179

Head East	185
30 Australia & Japan	187
31 Canadia	193
32 Somewhere Over a Rainbow	201
33 Barcelona, Busan, Beyond	213
34 The Ghost	223
35 Deadëye 2.0	227

About Black Patrick	245

BLACK PATRICK

"If I could, I would."
—Black Patrick

INTRODUCTION

FUCK YOU. WE ARE FUCKED. WE'RE FUCKING DOOMED. We live in a miserable time. There's zero chance. No hope. We have been bought and sold by demons. The demons are not some kind of imaginary beings from young adult novels. Real demons are a branch or two away from you on what you're led to believe is your family tree.

The only job we have—and that includes you, you miserable old fuck—is to preserve the planet for ourselves and our posterity. If you don't know that posterity word or its meaning you're a fucking asshole.

The Constitution of the United States of America

We the People of the United States, in Order to form a more perfect Union, establish Justice, insure domestic Tranquility, provide for the common defence, promote the general Welfare, and secure the Blessings of Liberty to ourselves and our Posterity, do ordain and establish this Constitution for the United States of America.

So, fuck you. We have an indispensable duty to the children of the children of your grandchildren. They get to live on a planet with food, water, air—shit like that. Sadly, for the descendants of the old fucks we're surrounded with today, the "special ones," the stupid old fucks, chose to void the social contract and fuck everything up. Brainwashed to the hilt, today's septuagenarians and octogenarians made the conscious decision to swallow loads and loads of infected cum blasting out of flaccid corporate cocks preaching stock market returns above everything else. Those sexy portfolios, growing and throbbing all around them—amazing in their lubriciousness.

The lazy fucks were handed a golden opportunity and they fucked it in the ass. And we fucked up by failing to hold those cunts accountable for crimes against humanity including generational theft, endless wars, poison for food, shitty education, non-existent transportation, the prison-incarceration industry...

Fuck you.

"You take and take and take and you keep and keep and keep!" those who preached nothing but greed said to their sheep.

How did that work out for you elderly fuckheads? Old, alone, miserable, without a friend other than your crooked financial advisor?

If you're lucky, you won't live long enough to see your children and grandchildren migrate toward the North Pole alongside the Central Americans your greed murdered to maintain that 23-cent banana price at Trader fucking Joe's.

Pro tip: pray your children and grandchildren are climate migrants. Economic factors drive migrants. Climate <u>refugees</u> will leave Orange County because of something you've undoubtedly encouraged and benefitted from—WAR! Bombs falling from the sky. So much fun! You don't want to be around when the miserable Orange County cunts are blown up and burnt to a crisp by barrel bombs and bootleg flamethrower drones built in that fucked up place the hillbilly electric car cunt pretends to launch habitable spaceships from. Fuck that guy and fuck anyone who knows that dogshit motherfucking loser who isn't using that punchable face as a human toilet or a target for archery practice.

Black Patrick says, "Fuck those people. They're no fun and they're evil."

ONE
SOMETIMES

1 NOTHING IS NOT EASY

DEADËYE DIDN'T LIKE THE QUESTION. "Why do we do this? Why do we do this? Are you fucking kidding me? We do this because we can't do anything else. We do this because we won't do anything else. We never even think about doing anything else. We rock 'n' roll until we die!"

"How do we make money?" Garth asked.

"We sell drugs. Next question."

"Who do we sell drugs to? We usually buy drugs. How can we sell drugs when we buy drugs from everyone we know?"

"Are you paying attention? We only sell drugs to strippers and hookers. Next question."

"Won't we blow all the money we make selling drugs to hookers and strippers on hookers and strippers?"

"I do."

"I'm not sure I understand your plan, Deadëye," Garth said, because drummers are much like cops and history teachers. They're stupid and they say a lot of stupid shit and they actually believe the stupid shit they say.

"The cartel fronted us a boatload of drugs—they like our band."

"What kind of drugs?"

"Every kind. I'll go alphabetically, from A to X: Adderall, cocaine, codeine, GHB, heroin, ketamine, LSD, MDMA, mescaline, methamphetamine, mushrooms, Norco, Oxycodone, PCP, Percocet, Valium, Vicodin, Xanax."

"What about weed?"

"We don't waste our time selling weed, Garth. You fucking burnout. Weed people are lame. This isn't 1989."

"How about crack?"

"Good idea. You can deal with the crackheads."

"I'm making a decent living flipping vintage gear, so I'm not sure I need to deal drugs."

"I'm not sure the world needs another pretentious little vintage gear twat walking the face of the Earth wasting our time babbling about vintage gear bullshit," Deadëye told Garth. "Know what I mean? Nobody is ever impressed by your knowledge of ribbon microphones and alnico magnets."

"I am."

"That's why you don't get any pussy. When's the last time you sold a vintage stomp box to a hot stripper?"

"Never."

"I sold a shitload of Xanax to the smokin' hot hooker and her extremely grateful group of stripper friends across the hall from my place last night."

"How many?"

"Hookers or Xanax?"

"Both."

"Six strippers. 500 Xanax. And 500 Adderall. And a few ounces of ketamine, six ounces of crystal meth, and six ounces of blow."

"Whoa."

"I paid the cartel back for the drugs they fronted me and I've already tripled my investment. And I still have $500,000 worth of drugs left."

"Aren't you worried about getting busted?"

"When's the last time you heard about anybody getting busted for drugs in Los Angeles?"

"Good point."

"Look, we sell drugs to strippers and hookers exclusively and we're good."

"I'm in."

Deadëye laid out the business plan. "Everybody in the band rents an apartment in my building on a different floor, plus we rent the basement for our rehearsal studio. There are so many hookers and strippers in and out of the building, already, nobody will ever notice our customers coming and going."

"Sounds like you've given the idea some thought," smart guy, Garth, said.

"Thought? I just started selling drugs to strippers and hookers two weeks ago and I already have garbage bags full of cash hidden in the walls of my apartment. Pro tip: cash makes good soundproofing material."

"How do we launder the money?"

"Merch. We inflate T-shirt sales figures and dump cash in the bank in every city we play a show."

"How do we smuggle drugs all over the country?"

"We don't. Strippers and hookers will travel to Los Angeles to hang out with us. Don't you know anything about FMTY?"

"No."

"That's when you pay a hooker from another city to visit. She offers Fly Me To You service."

"Is FMTY the same as BBBJCIM?"

"Usually. Anyway, after a couple of U.S. tours with multiple dates in stripper-heavy cities such as Vegas, Miami, Atlanta, Dallas, Houston, Portland, and New York, we'll have a solid client base of strippers. Hot strippers. After three years we never need to work again."

"What about Canada?"

"That's a great idea."

"We don't want to miss New Orleans. Or Chicago. And I've had remarkable luck in San Francisco, Orange County, San Diego, and Phoenix."

"You're cooking with gas, Garth. We need to do some research. There may be some big college towns in the South and Midwest loaded with hookers and strippers we haven't considered."

"What if we tried to find a hot stripper to be our bass player? For multiple reasons, including insider knowledge of the drug purchasing habits of today's most successful exotic dancers and highly-paid cocksuckers."

"Damn, that's an incredible idea. You know Lance is gay, right?"

"I do, now."

"That's a topic for another day. But a potential source of incremental sales revenue, big time. Anyway, I'll have two of whatever you had for breakfast. Put an ad on Craigslist looking for a new bass player. I'm still banned from Craigslist, so you'll have to do it."

"Do strippers still use Craigslist? Most of the ones I run into are on Facebook Marketplace or OfferUp."

"You're right. Put ads on those sites, too."

"How do you get banned from Craigslist, Lyft, and InstaCart? I don't know anybody who's ever been banned from even one of those websites."

"You left out Amazon. The short answer is, it's not easy. Nothing is not easy."

2. TRUCK STOPPERS

GARTH WAS SCARED SHITLESS AFTER HIS FIRST VISIT to a truck stop. "Those motherfuckers in the coffee shop wanted to kill me."

Deadëye didn't even look up from his mobile office on the table in the Deadëye tour bus.

"Did you hear me?" Garth asked, in a melodramatic fashion with a pained expression on his face.

"You forgot to take your clown makeup off, you fucking weirdo. We need a few more mirrors in this fucked-up traveling hell on wheels."

Why Garth decided to start wearing clown makeup escaped the rest of the band. Most drummers do stupid shit like drum rollercoasters or big gongs to get attention back there where nobody sees them. A dude in high heels, fishnets, and face paint in a truck stop may have been acceptable to previous generations of hillbillies, however, new hillbillies are much more sensitive. And a whole lot more stupid.

"Hillbillies used to be fun," Deadëye explained, "then they lost their sense of humor."

"There are some decent hillbilly comedians."

"Name one."

"Adam Carolla."

"Not at all funny."

"Rob Schneider."

"Super-lame super-creep. Both of those cunts live in Pasadena. Home of everything unfunny."

"Joe Rogan."

"I'll give you that one. Rogan's a really great stand-up comic, the rest of his bullshit is fucking lame. Who knew that, just by starting a podcast and morphing into a typical old, know-it-all, white guy hillbilly geezer cunt, Joe Rogan could become a billionaire?"

Deadëye returned to cooking the books and tried to concentrate on moving money around to confuse the Feds, but Garth was unhinged. The mental instability pervading the bus was palpable, so Deadëye interrupted his fictional accounting exercise to help out his pal. "Garth, we can't fix these fucks. We can't talk to them, we can't help them, we can't kill them. We travel the highways of America with a singular purpose—meet strippers and hookers. We avoid all contact with the baseball cap people, in as much as that is possible."

"Our best-selling item of merch is the Deadëye baseball cap."

"That's where you're wrong. Last night in Tempe we sold 65 Deadëye Eye Patches."

"Who the fuck is buying eye patches?"

"We promoted the show heavily on the Apache Nation Facebook. Bow and arrow accidents are rampant with the Apache these days. It's like a pandemic situation on the reservation."

"So, the Apache Nation's people are wearing eye patches to avoid arrows like the rest of us wore face masks to avoid COVID?"

"We don't know. We don't care. If the Apache Nation people believe our Kevlar eye patches will prevent arrows from decimating their eyeballs, that's great. We know they're bulletproof. We haven't tested any of the merch on arrows, yet."

"Maybe we need to rent a separate apartment to use as an indoor archery range."

"Garth, if you were a woman, I would kiss you right now."

"Did you just say we sold eye patches to the Apaches? Are you still smoking dope and watching Bugs Bunny?"

3 MAGIC BASS

As the sun rose over Durango, the woman in Deadëye's bed said, "When it's all lit up at night it looks like a giant gold mushroom cloud."

"Thanks, Magic, I appreciate that."

"I wasn't talking about you, Deadëye," Magic said. "It's not all about you."

"Is it about the acid?"

"I think so."

"You know, the planet is so well-designed to enslave us all these days, the only way to stop and appreciate the cool shit is with drugs."

"I agree, Deadëye, however, the world is changing so fast," Magic said. "It's hard to keep up with the prevailing trends."

"I read *Trends Journal*. How do you deal with the shifting winds of society?"

"I don't, but we have to stay ahead of the game. I take a trip to IKEA at least five or six times a year. On drugs. I've discovered downers don't work at all these days, for example. We need the speed/ketamine/Xanax combination right now. Now more than ever."

"Doesn't the combination of IKEA and ketamine kill your sex drive?"

"God no. I need so much cock when I snort ketamine—I can't get enough. Huge cocks. And lots of 'em. If I can't find cocks I need fists. I'm not ashamed to admit, I've turned to baseball bats, in a pinch."

"Perfect. You're hired. I'll let the rest of the band know we can stop looking for a bass player, now."

"Deadëye, you're the best."

"Thank God we got rid of that session bass player dude," Deadëye told Garth at breakfast one day.

"He keeps calling. He's really angry we left him in that brothel. There's practically no way out of Pahrump without a car. And that's not even the worst part."

"What's the worst part?" Deadëye asked.

"Lance is a gay man trapped in a brothel. He can't even enjoy being stranded there."

"Sucks to be him. Now we're a true power trio. As soon as we find out if our new bass player knows what to do with that other big instrument in her hands every night."

Garth must mean party pooper in every language. "We need a second guitarist and a real singer."

I'm going to kill that motherfucker one day. I'm going to kill him.

4 AVOCADO SEED SQUIRREL SITUATION

"DEADËYE, WHERE DID YOU GET THE SEED MONEY to get this punk rock enterprise off the ground?" nosy guy Garth asked.

"Nice choice of words. I did a shitload of acid one summer while studying at the horticulture school and created an avocado with a smaller seed. Hence, the seed money."

"The seed money came from smaller seeds?"

"Pretty much. Have you ever seen a squirrel eat an avocado?"

"No. But thanks for asking."

"A squirrel in an avocado tree chomps its way through the skin and fruit, the meat, if you will, of an avocado until it reaches the seed. And that's all the squirrel eats—the seed."

"That happened to me with a hooker in Medellin," Garth said.

"Makes sense. That's why people with penises go to Columbia."

"I went there for the cocaine."

"The point is, my avocado is the same size, but the seed inside is much smaller. So there's way more guacamole action per avocado."

"Why didn't farmers figure out how to do that a hundred years ago?"

"Farmers don't use the right drugs," Deadëye said. "All those farm fucks do is complain about shit and collect money from the government. It's a miracle we have any food to eat."

"Every farmer I know is a fucking moron."

"Garth, let me be the first to tell you. You are employee of the month."

"Awesome! If I'm an employee I can collect unemployment when you fire me."

"Dumbfuck, Deadëye doesn't fire people. He fires people," Deadëye said as he referred to himself in the third person and gestured toward his oversized outdoor pizza oven/incinerator. Like a psycho.

"You can't make me employee of the month and kill me at the same time."

"Wanna bet?"

5 TRAIN
TRAIN US TOUR

G ARTH REMAINED ETERNALLY CONFUSED. Because every person named Garth is an idiot. "Why are we touring on a train this time? Nobody does that."

"The only way to feel the noise is when it's good and loud," Deadëye answered.

"Do you feel the need to quote Motörhead lyrics every day because of some birth defect?" Garth asked Deadëye.

"Yes. We're carrying $1 million worth of narcotics. Try doing that through an airport."

"I thought you said $500,000."

"Inflation."

"What about a tour bus?"

"Think about it. Is there anything an inbred rural cop gets more excited about than a tour bus rolling down the interstate?"

"Yes. A school bus. A school bus full of high school junior varsity softball players."

"Whatever. Nobody gives a fuck about trains. There's no X-ray/MRI/cavity search action at an Amtrak station. We hit town, jump off the train, stroll across the street to the bar, get hammered, then take an Uber to the venue—there's no bullshit."

"Who are we selling all of the drugs to?"

"Hookers and strippers in Las Vegas. All of the drugs will be sold in the first week, then we don't have to be paranoid weirdos the rest of the tour."

"What do we do with all the cash we make selling drugs?"

"We buy vintage gear."

DEADËYE KNEW ENOUGH STRIPPERS in Las Vegas to unload all of the drugs hidden in the four inconspicuous-looking duffel bags he refused to let the staff at The Strat touch. In between visits to the Punk Rock Museum and the hospital, Deadëye unloaded the entire inventory in 72 hours.

Then Deadëye got a phone call. "I told you to call me."

"Fuck, dude, I'm so sorry. I honestly forgot. I swear I'll fix this. You tell me what you need and I'll make it happen."

"I need you to call me. Next time, call me."
"I will. I promise."
"I told you to call me."
"Who was that?" Garth asked.
"Just some dude I know. He runs some kind of Thailand-ish mafia thing in town. I think I'm going downstairs. If you and Magic wanna go home, it's all good. I'm on the road again! Next stop Provo!"

Just as the valet handed Deadëye the keys to the sprinter van, Garth arrived with a woman carrying a pot of coffee wearing nothing but a towel on her head and a hotel robe and dragging a half-zipped counterfeit Louis Vuitton bag behind her.

"Kingman, you moron. It's Kingman, not Provo."
"Kingmän. That's a great band name."
"I'm not going to Utah."
"Look, I said Provo in case there were listening devices in the room."
"The entire tour itinerary is online."
"I knew that."
"Are we in some kind of danger?"
"A little."
"That's hot," Magic said, and she wasn't talking about the coffee.
"We need to stop at a few guitar stores and a couple of banks," Deadëye said as he curbed the sprinter van on the way out of the hotel parking lot. "I brought ski masks."

6 SIX SIX SIX US TOUR

MAGIC SPENT MOST DAYS in her private train compartment while Garth and Deadëye held court in the dining car. "What are you reading?" Deadëye asked as he intruded upon Magic's solitude.

"It's fiction. You wouldn't understand. Men don't read fiction."

"I used to read fiction novels if you consider Hunter S. Thompson fiction. And Phillip K. Dick. If there isn't an initial in an author's name the book's gonna suck."

"I mostly read YA Fiction, so any author is okay since there's already a couple of initials in the category."

"What is YA Fiction?"

"Young adult fiction. Coming-of-age stories for young adults."

"Oh, I've seen some movies about that. *Barely Legal*—"

"No, stupid. Young adult meaning teenagers, pre-teens, older kids."

"So, it's called 'Young Adult' (air quotes) but it's for children? Who's the pervert who came up with that brilliant idea?"

"What the fuck else would they call it?"

"Fiction?" Deadëye posited. "Fiction for adolescents? All I know is, when I was an adolescent, I wouldn't have read anything labeled 'young adult' (air quotes, again) I was reading *Kerrang!* and Tolstoy."

"You skipped your childhood. Sucks for you."

"Who invented YA fiction?"

"S.E. Hinton."

T HE TOUR SLOWLY WORKED ITS WAY through America without purpose until Deadëye, the band, reached Miami.

"What a toilet," Garth said to Deadëye. "This town is total bullshit."

"No kidding," Deadëye said. "Florida is one big toilet and Miami is a toilet within a toilet."

"How do we fuck with these people here? Can we drive around town on a flatbed truck murdering the fuckers with our sound, again?"

"No, we're going on a cruise."

"A cruise?" Garth squealed. "The last time I went on a cruise I got MRSA pneumonia and had to be airlifted in a helicopter from the Gulf of Mexico to Houston."

"That won't happen this time."

"The doctors told me the only way I might possibly survive was if they put me in a medically-induced coma and pumped me full of antibiotics."

"That's not happening this time."

"I was in a coma for six months! Awake the entire time! But I couldn't speak or move at all! I heard everything! Some of those nurses are not nice people."

"Garth, we're not taking a cruise ship filled with near-death geezers anywhere. We're cruising up the Intracoastal Waterway from Miami to Boston. I bought a fucking yacht."

"Isn't it hurricane season?" Garth asked.

"We need to learn that Scorpions song."

"I'm a good whistler," Garth offered.

"Not that one, dumbass. The one about the hurricane."

D EADËYE COULDN'T KEEP A SECRET. "I have good news, Magic. I bought a yacht and we're doing a two-week tour of the East Coast without ever leaving the boat."

"Yacht rock?"

"Fuck, yeah. We're claiming the genre for Deadëye, for the 21st century. There are no contemporary yacht rockers."

"Yachts are for douchebags."

"We know that. That's why it'll be so much fun cruising up the Intracoastal Waterway all the way from Miami to Boston murdering the cunts with boats and docks and soon-to-be-underwater waterfront mansions with our sound. And the pyro. And our T-shirt cannons. You're gonna need more amps."

"I hate boats."

"Me too. But this one has five bedrooms, six-and-a-half baths, two kitchens, a washer and dryer—it's way nicer than any place I've ever lived."

"Does it have a stage?"

"The *SS Deadëye* has a massive deck we're using as a stage."

7 FISTING THE F.B.I.

"THE F.B.I. IS HERE," Garth announced.

"I wonder why?" Deadëye asked, sarcastically.

"Holy fuck! We're all going to prison!" Magic squealed in a panic.

A stereotypical former high school athlete with 'roid rage and a shaved head said, "Look, Mr. Deadëye, we don't care about your personal drugs or hookers or strippers or gambling bullshit problems." Special Agent Mendoza continued, "But when every hooker and stripper in Las Vegas calls us we can't really ignore that."

"Why would every stripper and hooker call the F.B.I.?" Deadëye asked the enemy of all things fun.

"Every hooker, stripper, pimp, drug dealer, and professional athlete in Las Vegas is a confidential informant."

"Good to know, officer. What did they say about us?"

"Your ketamine is amazing. You know what that means."

"No. Not really."

"It means everybody in Las Vegas is fisting. Fisting like there's no tomorrow."

"Everybody?"

"Everybody. Everybody. The whole town is shut down. All anybody wants to do is get fisted. If this continues, the entire gambling industry collapses and Carrot Top returns to the road."

"Dude, you can't blame us for that cunt's escape from Las Vegas. We only brought 50 pounds of ketamine with us on this trip."

"Only fifty pounds? That's enough ketamine to keep fisters and fistees busy for a year. That'll destroy the entire economy of Nevada and Utah."

"Utah?"

"Utah. Big time. A lot of slow-pitch softball pitchers in Salt Lake City. And almost as many catchers. Anyway, fisting is awesome, however, it's not a great idea to be on the receiving end more than a couple of times a year."

"That's not what the nurse told me when I saw her through the face hole in the milking table. I have to admit, by the time the proctologist finished fisting me, I was a new man. Maybe because she kept calling me Pedro while she violently invaded my rectum with her cute little hand. I'm pretty sure she made it all the way to her shoulder by the time the session was done."

"Just stop right there."

"I'm not sure why they brought in all of those nursing students from the community college. Their enthusiastic applause, cheers, and chants seemed to motivate the doctor."

"Are you okay? Do you need to go to the hospital?"

"Yes and yes."

WHILE EVERYBODY ELSE in his life wasted his time talking about how great things used to be, all Deadëye could think about was the future. When Deadëye finally found the right dock he met boat captain Doc.

"What makes you think you can skipper our stupidly expensive boat?" Deadëye asked the man dressed like the Skipper from Gilligan's Island.

"What makes you think you're worth a minute of my time, cocksucker?" Doc asked.

"Where the fuck is the boat?" Deadëye asked. "Let's get this motherfucking party started."

8 YACHT ROCK

Deadëye and company walked into the yacht's galley, and liked what they saw, then Deadëye killed the vibe. "CPA Chris says we need to record an album. Our business doesn't look legit unless we're recording and releasing albums."

"What the fuck does that guy know?" Magic asked.

Deadëye responded, somewhat belligerently, "He knows how to keep you, and you, and me out of prison!"

Garth said, "I've written a couple of new songs."

"Save that garbage for your solo project."

"Dude, I just wanna go back to Huntington Beach," Garth confessed. "I worked at Vons, had a quiet life, nobody ever challenged me intellectually…"

"Fuck. I'll send your stupid fucking ass back to that cowtown right fucking now. I went to high school in that shithole of a dump. There isn't a motherfucking thing of any value in Huntington Beach. Those cunts think they're so fucking special. We need to build a wall around that hellhole and see how long it takes until they realize they don't have shit, they don't know shit, and they don't do shit. Huntington Beach people are worth nothing, they contribute nothing, they sit around and bitch and moan and talk about how much better they are. Let 'em starve. Fuck those good-for-nothing motherfucking losers."

"They're not all bad."

"Yes, they fucking are. You're done. Get ready to get the fuck off my tugboat."

Deadëye gave Garth a $5,000 parting gift and called him an Uber. He told the Uber guy to take Garth to the airport, got back on the boat, and threw Garth's drums in the river as the Hyundai Sonata drove that cunt away. "Fuck that guy."

"I'M GLAD YOU FINALLY GOT RID OF THAT CREEPY fucking weirdo," Magic said as she launched a ride cymbal like a frisbee into the brackish waters of the Intracoastal stage channel. "Garth told me he has three kids in Orange County, each with different cousins."

"His family tree has no branches," Deadëye added as he blasted Garth's floor tom with a shotgun to help it sink faster.

"I'm learning so much on this tour," Magic told Deadëye right before she kicked a kick drum off the side of the *SS Deadëye*. "I thought I already knew everything."

"Where are you from?"

"Newport Beach."

"Aw, fuck," Deadëye said. "You're fired."

"What! Why?"

"Look, I know you think you're special—you're different! But all of you Orange County cunts are the same. I'm not saying there's anything wrong with that. However, it's still a free country, unless you want a library book in Huntington Beach, so I'm exercising my freedom of choice and telling you to get the fuck off of my boat right fucking now."

"That's racist!"

"Not really. I think it's more bigoted. Call me a bigot, I don't care. All I know is I won't waste a single minute of the time I have left on this planet with myopic Orange County people. Call the Jesse Jackson of Orange County's oppressed white fucks and have me canceled. I. Don't. Care."

"I hate you, Deadëye!" screamed the woman whose name had already been forgotten.

"C'mon, you're a better swimmer than that!"

And that's how Deadëye the band became Deadëye the solo artist. Never go on a cruise with a band. I think Jimmy Bain said that. He may have been the last in line at the buffet one day.

9 NEW BAND

THE MUSIC SCENE IN CHARLESTON LOOKED BLEAK, at first glance. The first place Deadëye landed struck him as the typical Live Nation plantation situation—owned by assholes, managed by robots, featuring shitty bands in a shittier atmosphere. The venue was half-full, and, despite the miserable Mall-of-America vibe, the band on stage was pretty great—a three-piece all-female screamo situation. As Deadëye contemplated his options for the evening the emo band's drummer sat down at the bar a couple of stools away and ordered three pitchers of margaritas.

"You guys were great," Deadëye told the drummer.

"We sucked," she said. "That was our last show."

"What's next?"

"Back to Starbucks, for me. The other bitches are strippers, so they don't really care. It's a travesty how those whores make more money eating man foam than I make selling oat milk foam."

"Why don't we combine the two? I need a bass player and a drummer right now."

"Who are you."

"I'm Deadëye, who are you?"

"I'm Fiona," said Fiona as she eyed Deadëye suspiciously. "Do you call yourself Deadëye so women will stare deeply into your mesmerizing blue eyes and search for the dead eye?"

"I do now."

"Let's go to the back, I need to load out."

Backstage the band declared victory and loaded their van with gear. Fiona introduced Deadëye to Tammy, the bass player, and Amber, the screaming guitar player. "You can't quit now," Deadëye said.

"We just did," Tammy said.

"The music business is bullshit," Amber added. "Only morons believe there's a future in music."

Deadëye nodded in agreement and wondered aloud, "Yeah, but what's a future?"

F IONA, TAMMY, AND AMBER'S BAND were called Emo Strippers on Acid. "What kind of hellhole is this town?" Deadëye asked. "Why wasn't this place packed?"

"Live Nation are pussies," Amber said. "They were afraid to include us in any advertising."

"What do you think about Deadëye and the Emo Strippers on Acid?" Deadëye asked his new friends. "I have a tour boat."

"A tour boat?" Amber asked.

"Yes. A tour boat. It's a lot bigger than a tour bus and it has a built-in stage."

"Whatever," Tammy said, "we're going to the pinball bar down the street. If you can figure out where it is and get there we might talk to you, creep."

That wasn't very nice, Deadëye thought. *I don't wanna waste my time with assholes. But I probably would have told me to fuck off, too, so maybe I should find that bullshit hipster pinball place. In an hour. Deadëye doesn't ever look desperate.*

"There he is," Amber exclaimed as Deadëye walked in the door of the pinball bar. The emo trio all shared a laugh at Deadëye's expense as Amber said, "I told you he's desperate!"

Fiona continued the abuse, "Did you sail over here on your tour boat?"

"Fiona," Deadëye started, ready to land a fatal blow to her self-esteem, until he stopped himself. "I love your snare sound. It sounds like a firecracker every time you slam the shit out of it."

"Really?"

"Really. It cuts through everything. Through walls. Floors. I heard it a block away from the venue."

"Thanks."

"I have a gig in Myrtle Beach in four days, then a show in Wilmington, then Norfolk, then Richmond, and some other stuff."

"On your tour boat?" Amber asked.

"As a matter of fact, yes."

"I don't believe you," Tammy said.

"I get it. I wouldn't believe me either," Deadëye admitted. "Check my Instagram out and call me if you wanna come see the infamous tour boat. I'll be in town for a couple of days."

"Okay, Deadëye. What's your Instagram."

Because he couldn't help it, Deadëye said, "If you can figure out where it is and get there I might talk to you, creeps."

D EADËYE DIDN'T HEAR FROM ANY Emo Strippers on Acid, so the next evening he returned to the scene of the pinball bar massacre.

"You shouldn't come here by yourself," the woman cloaked in darkness growled in his ear. "You look desperate."

"Hey," Deadëye said without a hint of enthusiasm when he realized Amber was the one insulting him.

"Somebody hacked your Instagram account," Amber reported. "Or you're not real. We tried to find you but we couldn't."

"Let's go," Deadëye said. "Right now. To the boat."

"Are you driving?"

"No, the boat's 10 minutes away. We can walk."

Alone without the armor her bandmates and the familiar situation pinball machines provided, Amber's more apprehensive and guarded persona beguiled Deadëye. Not what he expected from an Emo Stripper on Acid. Deadëye asked Amber, "Where did you get that Destroyer? I'd kill to own one of those."

"Craigslist. Same place I met the other whores in the band."

"I should've known," Deadëye said. "Call Tammy and Fiona, tell them to bring their gear, and meet us at the boat. We can barbecue and play some music together. See if it works."

"Can I invite my boyfriend?"

"Sure, invite one of your sugar daddies."

"That's offensive."

"I know everything about you. Unless your Instagram was hacked, too."

"Ha."

Things were going great on the boat until Tammy revealed her veganism and horror at the steaks grilling aboard *SS Deadëye*. Deadëye summarily dismissed Tammy at which time Amber volunteered to move from guitar to bass.

"I'm done giving people second chances," Deadëye said as Tammy roared away in the band's van screaming and flashing some kind of gang signal out the window. "Life is too short. People never improve. Never."

"What's your plan, Deadëye?" Amber asked as Deadëye and the remaining Emo Strippers on Acid enjoyed hefty slabs of tender, young beef inside the boat. On acid. "We need to hear some of your music."

"I'll play you some music, that's the plan."

Deadëye fired up the YouTube, turned up the volume, and let loose with the shittiest footage he could find of his previous band. With expectations sufficiently lowered, he then navigated to the most recent, killer song he had recorded with his famous producer friend in the Los Angeles neighborhood he once called home. The Emo Stripper twins on acid simply stared at Deadëye.

"You finally met one you can't figure out, huh?"

Deadëye, Fiona, and Amber passed out as the sky began to turn less black and awoke to boat pilot Doc's return from his weekend off hunting ducks or whatever boat people do on days off.

"Your boat pilot is named Doc?" Amber asked before her hungover ass and their drummer burst into a ridiculous fit of hangover-assisted laughter.

"I'm making coffee," Doc said. "Y'all look rode hard and put away wet. We're leavin' in 20 minutes for Myrtle."

"Are we going with Doc?" Deadëye asked Fiona and Amber, who laughed hysterically and remained aboard the *SS Deadëye* as Charleston disappeared behind the boat into the soft morning light.

Fiona and Amber screamed, "Doc!" at random times for their entertainment. It's not against the law.

"BUSINESS MEETING!" DEADËYE DECLARED as the rest of his band regained consciousness. "I'm hiring you two for two weeks to do this run of shows. We rehearse for three days, play shows every single day after that, and we're done. How much money do you want?"

"We didn't pack for this trip," Amber said. "So, first, you need to take us shopping and buy us clothes and makeup and everything else."

Fiona added, "I need $500 a day or I'm going home."

"$300 each per day, you never pay for anything, we split all of the money we make equally. We're a team."

"$2,500 per week or I'm out," Fiona said.

Deadëye said, "I'll be right back."

"You play the tuba?" Amber asked as Deadëye returned with a giant instrument case.

"No, this is where I keep the petty cash," Deadëye said as he opened the tuba case full of $100 bills. "Take ten grand each. Let me know when you need more."

Deadëye decided against recruiting Fiona and Amber into his drug smuggling and money laundering scheme, for the moment. "We have a couple of days to learn ten songs."

Amber said, "We're stopping in Georgetown to go shopping for basic shit. Give Fiona your credit card so she can pay for the things we're ordering online."

Deadëye lost track of time thanks to all of the hallucinogens Amber found in the tuba case.

"Holy shit! We have a show tomorrow!" Deadëye screamed at the rainbow-colored fighter jets flying in and out of the carbonated ocean waters their boat was flying over.

"We already know all your songs," the giant panda bear named Amber Panda said.

"How?" Deadëye asked.

"We found your set list in the tuba case," the ghost of Fiona said.

"Then we found the songs online," Arnold Schwarzenegger said.

"Then we learned them," Billy Barty announced.

"Do they suck?"

"Yes, they sucked. They did suck. They don't suck anymore."

"Myrtle Beach is a trip," Deadëye told Doc one day. "This whole part of the planet is bizarre."

"What makes you say that?"

"We're taking a yacht to Guitar Center."

"That's because you fucked up and didn't buy the yacht with the helipad."

"Be honest," Deadëye said to Doc, "are these the right people for my band? They're really fun, and super hot, but I haven't even heard 'em play a note of my music."

"I have," Doc said. "They're really fucking serious. Fiona and Amber have spent hours and hours on your songs —they know 'em better than you."

"I had no idea."

"You need to put your fucking gear up there on the roof and turn that shit up."

"Where? Where do we do that?"

"Here." Doc pointed across the street from the yacht's berth at a giant musical instrument store. "Get off my boat. Go clean out Guitar Center. When you get back I'll have all of your gear set up and ready to go on the roof."

"You know how to do that?"

"You blast through four songs at high volume and we get the fuck outta here—the pigs will confiscate your amps, guitars, drums, and women around here."

"It's a good thing I don't have any women around here."

Doc rang a bell and screamed, "Get the fuck off my vessel!" over the intercom system. Fiona, Amber, and Deadëye walked a plank to a dock and across the street into America's sole remaining bastion of guitar predictability.

"The leads are weak," Fiona said.

Deadëye's hypersensitivity about his uninspired guitar solo action ignited his entire suddenly nervous nervous system. "Fuck you, Fiona."

The dumbass Turnstile fan working the turnstile in the Guitar Center foyer looked as dumb as a Myrtle Beach moron ever could. Perhaps Deadëye's bigotry toward drooling morbidly obese fucks adorned in cute little security guard outfits clouded the valuation of his fellow human being. Whatever. A dirty look and a grunt never stopped Deadëye from testing a Marshall stack in a Guitar Center.

The trio split up, temporarily, and explored the Walmart of guitar stores. Deadëye checked out the used guitars and amps. Because Guitar Center personnel are stupid, and don't know what the fuck they're doing, they often undervalue gear in amazing ways.

With no amazing deals evident and a million better things to do, the Deadëye crew picked up some accessories and bid adieu to the Guitar Center crew.

"I need drugs," Deadëye said as the power trio of all power trios left the retail power center via the sidewalk in front of Five Guys.

Fiona volunteered, "I really need some ketamine," as she twirled her newly-acquired beefy drumsticks and shook maracas seductively.

Deadëye had to admit, "I might have enough acid, mushrooms, and MDMA to last a couple of weeks, but I'm dead if we run out of Adderall and Xanax."

"We need ketamine!" Amber screamed as the trio approached the *SS Deadëye*.

"Now you tell me," eavesdropper Doc said from his perch on the bow. As he assisted the ladies aboard the cruising vessel, he told the band, in a hushed tone, "My daughter does anesthesia at the hospital here in town. She's comin' over with a big bag of ketamine and a jug of cough syrup."

"What about—" Amber started to ask, before she was cut off by the captain.

"Listen, ladies. We have every mind-altering chemical you can imagine on this boat. If there's something else you need and you don't wanna pay for it, you know what to do."

"Go to the hospital?"

"That's not the international sign language for that," Deadëye said.

"I'm not sucking Doc's cock," Amber announced. "Again."

Deadëye asked Doc, "Do you think we should rehearse before the first show?"

"Did Howlin' Wolf ever rehearse?" Doc answered with a question.

"Fuck yeah, Howlin' Wolf rehearsed," Deadëye told Doc. "Howlin' Wolf was a fucking professional in every way."

"Well. you're no Howlin' Wolf, so don't waste any time rehearsing."

"I want to be in a normal band. Where everyone's happy. Deadëye, make me a rock star."

"Get the fuck off me," Deadëye told Fiona. "I'm a happily ex-married man."

"Sorry."

"And, besides, you're a drummer. And you don't have big tits."

That was a dirty trick. And it worked. Deadëye had always wanted to see Fiona's rack. Almost as much as Fiona had dreamed about staring at Deadëye's cock before she covered it with her saliva and made it disappear into a number of places. Almost.

"Why is everybody getting laid but me?" Deadëye asked Amber. "I'm the star here. What the fuck?"

"Enjoy it while it lasts. I am the star. I will be in front and you will be in back."

"I accept your challenge, Amber. Musically and sexually. Healthy competition and a couple of hours of cardio three times a week will only make both of us better."

"Fuck you, motherfucker. I'm here every fucking day packing a hatchet, a shovel, and a plan to make you disappear."

"Amber, you stupid cunt. In America, we use guns." And that's the last time anybody heard a word out of Amber. Orlando's Las Vegas Cambodian mafia outpost crew set the crime scene and nobody noticed returned band member Magic looked almost exactly like Amber. Goth girls are a lot like big, fat, stupid bikers—desperate to express their individuality by looking the same as each other.

"Did you kill Amber?"

"Doc, that's really rude. The body isn't even cold, yet."

"So that's why you always travel with that infrared thermometer thing."

"Sorta. It sees through walls, too."

10 EAST COAST TOUR

ONCE HER DEPROGRAMMING WAS COMPLETE, Magic assumed many positions on the *SS Deadëye* and became an Emo Stripper on Acid just in time to perform at the band's first show in Virginia—Magic was ready, but the world wasn't ready for Deadëye and the Emo Strippers on Acid. So the band was overcome with emotion when the kind people of Richmond, Virginia embraced the band as one of their own.

"What's wrong Deadëye, too much pussy?" Doc asked Deadëye the following afternoon.

"My accountant keeps saying we need to record a new album."

"Why?"

"I've told you a dozen times. This is supposed to look like a legitimate business."

For whatever reason, Doc laughed so uncontrollably snot shot out of his nose and marine life scattered. Once he regained control of most of his orifices, Doc said, "I know a guy."

"Ladies, I have fantastic news. We're recording an album together."

"Really?"

"Really. I just booked the studio. All we need to do is write a dozen new songs."

"We have a hundred."

"Pick the best seven. Let's eat mushrooms. Play 'em live at full volume."

"We need cocaine."

11 JAMAICA

Nothing good ever happened when Doc joined Deadëye in the party shower behind the salon. Except for that one time Deadëye and Doc agreed to forget and deny.

"A man named Eyeball called," Doc said as Deadëye handed him a loofa. "His record store burned to the ground."

"Again? Man, that sucks. Fire tornado?"

"No, Eyeball said somebody at the skateboard shop used a George Foreman Grill to make coffee."

"What year is this? That sounds like a tough one to explain to an insurance adjuster."

"Apparently not. Eyeball collected $4.2 million from Warren Buffett's organized crime family's insurance biz Gestapo fucks. Do you wanna know what he did as soon as he cashed the insurance check?"

"No. I already know. I hope it was a mule instead of a donkey this time."

"He bought the skateboard shop a new George Foreman Grill. Anyway, now he wants to start a record company. He wants to sign Dead—"

"Fuck that guy. We have enough problems without Eyeball around. I swear to God, the first day that fucker is on a boat he'll disappear underwater wearing a diving mask and a snorkel. Five minutes after that he'll surface with a dozen baby dolphins pre-skewered on those underwater Apache sticks."

Underwater Apache sticks? "Arrows?" Doc asked in a state of bewilderment. *Jesus fucking Christ.* Always the professional, the man whose eyes never left the prize asked Deadëye, "So, you don't wanna be big in Japan?"

"Not with that clown."

Like Kenny Rogers, Doc knew some things, including:
- When to walk away.
- When to run. To the exact center of the Bermuda Triangle.

"Deadëye, I thought, this time, things would be different. I've been a seaman my whole life—"

"Haven't we all?"

"—and, as hard as I try, I can't understand your kind."

Deadëye almost told Doc to eat shit and die, but he paused just long enough to say, "Doc-man, we need to go see a man in Jamaica. When he was one of us, he went by the name of the name of Johnny Cash."

After rivers of tears and too much painful-to-watch male bonding, the motorboaters informed the motorboatees of the tour's detour.

Where Fiona received her information and kept a hospital's worth of first aid equipment nobody ever figured out. "It's a good thing I brought my own rape kit. Jamaica is the last place on Earth I would ever visit voluntarily. Even Johnny Cash lived in Haiti."

Why Deadëye found it necessary to use the ship's intercom to summon the spirit of the deceased Kenny Rogers to the bridge at that moment is another mystery best left unexplored. Columbus probably did a lot of shit like that, too.

"How far is Jamaica from Virginia, anyway?" Deadëye asked Doc.

"Eight days," Doc answered. "We need to stop and pick up my first mate and engineer in St. Augustine. We'll have the boat serviced and inspected, spend some time getting the crew acquainted there, then, it's four days to Jamaica."

"Cool."

"We'll spend a couple of days in Jamaica then haul ass to Manhattan. You don't need to waste any time in D.C. or Jersey. A couple of laps around Manhattan then we hit the Hudson until we arrive in Kingston. I'll send the crew home from New York."

"Sounds like you have a plan, Doc," Deadëye said. "What's after that?"

"10 days in the studio with the ladies, max. Then you send 'em home and mix the record."

"Okay."

"Then, you get the LP mastered and the vinyl pressed. While that's happening we're setting it all up—press, planning the tour, all that shit."

"Right."

"And, while we're at the studio in West Hurley, you record a solo acoustic record, we press a bunch of vinyl, CDs, cassettes, print some T-shirts, whatever, jump in a van, and woodshed it all the way back across the US of fuckin' A to Los Angeles."

"What about the boat?"

"I already have a buyer. $1 million more than you paid for it."

"Fuck it. Let's do it."

THE CAST AND CREW ONBOARD *SS DEADËYE* were up for the challenge. Richmond validated the band's potential, and that's all anybody ever needs.

Without any onshore distractions, save for a couple of days exploring the prehistoric star fort in St. Augustine, Deadëye and the Emo Strippers on Acid devoted most waking hours to rehearsals for the post-Johnny Cash excursion's recording sessions. Alarm clocks sounded at 1:43 p.m. daily for breakfast, and, every evening at 1:43 a.m., when the band and Doc retired to the Captain's Quarters for an hour of Johnny Cash music, video, literature, and education carefully crafted and delivered via Captain Doc.

"Why do we schedule shit at 1:32? That's such a random time."

"It's 1:43, Fiona. When you schedule shit at a very specific time people know you're serious and you'll murder them if they waste a minute of your time. On another topic, let's take time for a microsecond of silence to remember our departed bandmate, Angela."

"It's Amber."

"Whatever, let's continue, Doc."

"Fiona, you ask all the right questions. The last song Johnny Cash recorded was *Engine One-Forty-Three*, recorded shortly before he died in 2003. The year before you were born."

"Now I know, thank you, Doc," Fiona said, angrily turning her scowl toward Deadëye. "You didn't have to be such a dick about it, Deadëye."

Maybe Fiona was right, Deadëye wondered, as a sword-wielding scuba diver emerged from the warm waters of the Caribbean and hacked off Fiona's head, arms, legs, and penis. *And maybe Deadëye and the Cambodian Death Squad is a better name for a band, now that a third of the band—the new, self-appointed, assassin/drummer—is a hot stripper from Phnom Penh. Note to self: even while murdering, we are all networking.*

"Sonyta, may I borrow your machete?"

Sonyta handed Deadëye her big knife, which launched itself into the waters of the Caribbean. "We're done killing."

"Speak for yourself, motherfucker. I dug that sacred sword out of the skull-filled soil of Angkor Wat."

"Drop a pin, you can come back and get it later. Anyway, do you believe you have what it takes to be an Emo Stripper on Acid?"

DEADËYE WOKE UP THE AFTERNOON after Fiona, like those Space Shuttle astronauts, fed the fish. "Man, it's too bad Fiona and Amber got abducted by those pirates off Haiti. Should we call someone?"

"Watch out, this shit will peel your skin," Doc said through his hazmat suit as he pressure-washed the scene of an unreported crime with a solution of lemon-scented bleach and ammonia.

"It smells like my childhood in Cambodia," Sonyta announced as she appeared in an itsy-bitsy-teeny-weeny-litttle-tiny-pink-bikini.

"I need a respirator," Doc declared.

On the sundeck of the moored *SS Deadëye*, Deadëye delivered the 411 to Sonyta. "Ya know, the life expectancy of an Emo Stripper on Acid isn't very long."

"I'm from Cambodia."

"You keep saying that, and I believe you," Deadëye said. "But we need to make you more of an emo stripper and less of a Cambodian stripper. How do we do that?"

"Pay for my sister's kid to go to college."

"How much will that cost?"

"75 cents per day."

Deadëye did the math and asked, "How about I just give you five thousand dollars right now?"

"Yes. Now I can tell my sister to cancel the abortion."

"Wow. That sounds a little extreme."

"If you said no I was going to ask you for $50 for the abortion."

Doc finished pressure-washing the decks of the yacht with chemical weapons and joined Deadëye and Sonyta at the bar in the salon. "Your new bass player has a heroin problem," he announced. "Maybe she'll wake up, maybe she won't."

"Aw, fuck," Deadëye said as he laid his face on the bar Doc had just disinfected. "Where do we find another bass player/Emo Stripper on Acid again on such short notice?"

Well, it turns out, 5% of the goth hookers on the internet moonlight as strippers. And half of the hot ones play bass.

12 FIRE TORNADO RECORDS

Deadëye elected Eyeball to run the Deadëye record and merchandise enterprise, named Fire Tornado Records. Eyeball appointed his trusted and worthy pal, Dennis, to run the record store empire, which was absorbed within the Deadëye conglomeration of rock 'n' roll madness.

During Eyeball's employee orientation on mescaline, Deadëye paused and asked Eyeball, "I wonder if Dennis is the guy who ran that Tower Records in Anaheim when my grandpa sawed a hole in the roof and stole a thousand CDs."

"He probably was."

"My earliest memories are of Grandpa taking me shopping for costumes at the Halloween store where he said Tower Records used to be. Every year, he would point at the ceiling above the princess outfits and tell me the story of how he and his buddy used a reciprocating saw to cut a hole in the roof and steal a bunch of easily laundered contraband. Then he'd tell me how they fucked up and forgot to bring a ladder. Or a rope. So they held on to the ripped-apart roofing around the hole until it collapsed under their weight and dropped them into the store."

"Sounds like it worked, then."

"Not really. They brought a dozen big, black trash bags, filled them with CDs, and, only after the bags were full, discovered there was no way out."

"What?"

"The back doors were made of steel with steel bars. The windows and glass doors on the front of the building had security gates made out of steel."

"What did they do?"

"They found a ladder, but it wasn't tall enough to reach the hole in the roof."

"Wow."

"So they piled up a bunch of boxes of shit from the Classical section, used that mountain of garbage to increase the height of the ladder, and barely escaped before the cops showed up."

"Weren't there cops all over the place looking for 'em?"

"Yeah, dozens. Roberto and my grandpa whipped out leaf blowers and lawnmowers and fucked around at the Chinese restaurant next door for a while and then drove away in a pickup truck full of CDs. The cops never suspected them. They never even talked to them! There's something to be said for being invisible people."

"Deadëye and the Invisible People: *There's Something to be Said*."

"Eyeball, that's a great idea."

NOT EVEN A WEEK INTO HIS JOB running Deadëye Records, Eyeball was already causing problems. "Fiona wants Amber to come back and play bass but Amber plays guitar and sings better than you so they really want you out."

Deadëye said, "I thought we killed Fiona and Amber. You'd have to write my name in cocaine to make me spend another minute of my life with Amber. Or Fiona. And somebody would need to find all of their parts and pieces, sew 'em back together, and reanimate their corpses before that."

The funny thing was, Eyeball didn't know Deadëye's last name, so he didn't buy nearly enough drugs to write Wolfeschlegelsteinhausenbergerdorff in cocaine.

The ever-sensitive Deadëye sensed distress within his treasured bandmate and partner in crime. "Dude, what the fuck?" may not have been the best way to initiate the conversation with Fiona. "I thought you were dead. No more LSD for me."

The more diplomatic Fiona told Deadëye, "The leads are weak. The leads are weak."

"My leads are weak?"

"Yes."

"Fiona, you're right," Deadëye confessed. "My leads are weak. And my grandma always told me, be a bass player, be a bass player."

"The same way Filipino grandmas tell their kids to be nurses?"

"Exactly. Fiona, take my guitar. Magic is the goth Yngwie Whatshisname. I am the bass player now."

"Who's Magic?"

"Sonyta's friend. She's here somewhere."

"Thank God. Are you still the singer?"

"Yes."

"Oh."

"Sensei say, the sidewalk is the ceiling to the underworld."

13 SOLID LINEUP

THE CRUISE FROM FLORIDA to Jamaica allowed Sonyta, Magic, and Deadëye to form a rock 'n' roll bond after Sonyta killed Amber and Fiona again. Like a three-engined jet, Deadëye, the power trio, roared across the Caribbean picking up speed and gaining altitude. By the time *SS Deadëye* hit Manchego Cheese Bay, the band had a dozen songs ready to record.

"Get the ladies in shape to knock out the basic tracks in three days so you can get rid of 'em and spend a week on guitar overdubs, vocals, and weird shit," Doc advised.

"I'll think about it," Deadëye said. "Last time you said ten days."

"Last time I'd only pressure-washed the deck once. Get the basic tracks done and send those bitches home. That's what Johnny Cash would do."

Deadëye slowly realized Doc was more than an Intracoastal navigator. He was a guru. A source of wisdom. Perhaps, even, a time-traveling Aztec God. For the first time in his life, Deadëye chose to relax, heed the advice, and allow someone else to take over the decision-making process.

"Doc, you know what Deadëye needs?"

"Yes."

"I, we, need a manager. Do you know anybody?"

"Yes, I did, but my godfather passed away thirty years ago. God rest his soul."

"Rest in peace. Who was your godfather?"

"Peter Grant."

"Fuck."

JAMAICA DESTROYED ALL PRETENSE AND EGO within the Deadëye crew. Overcome with emotion and inspiration, the band and its boat roared away from Jamaica ready to commit musical murder. Nobody wanted to talk, all anybody wanted to do was rock. Without any conversation or verbal communication, the new band of Emo Strippers on Acid was laser-focused, serious as a heart attack, and in sync. By the time they got to Manhattan, the razor-sharp audio assassins were on fire. Four laps around the island made fans of the breakfast, lunch, dinner, late night, and midnight crowds pummeled by the band's power. By the time they got to the nearest port to Woodstock, they were half a million strong. In their minds.

14
WELCOME TO WEST HURLEY

S ONYTA WAS AMPED. "Fuck yeah! Let's get this party started."

"Where's my fucking amp? I'm ready." Magic said as she echoed Sonyta's enthusiasm.

"This is your band. Get the fuck in there. You and me and Sonyta and Magic are equal partners," Peter Grant's godson, Doc, said. "No more drama, no more bullshit, we make records, we tour the world, we make history."

"Are you sure they're ready?"

"Not exactly. Go grab a burger and come back in an hour," Doc said.

Deadëye beat feet and hit the streets heading for the closest burger joint to eat meat. Five minutes down the highway and 20 minutes from his destination a man in a beat-up old pickup truck stopped in front of Deadëye.

"Are you lost?"

"Nope."

"Do ya need a ride?"

"Nope."

"Yes you do," the benevolent pickup truck driver said. "Get in."

As a stranger in a strange land, Deadëye dropped his guard and joined his possible murderer in a serial killer vehicle.

"What the fuck is wrong with you?" the local yokel asked Deadëye.

"It's a long list. Thanks for the lift. Who the fuck are you?"

"I'm Jason. I run a restaurant down the road near the reservoir."

"I wanted to go there, but you're closed on Tuesday."

"Don't be a dick here."

Jason introduced Deadëye to everybody he needed to know in the Woodstock area of wherever he was. Like Marin County, none of them were under 50-years-old.

"I gotta go," Deadëye told Jason.
"Need a ride?"
"No, I'm gonna run."

Deadëye ran back to the studio where Magic and Sonyta were rattling the rafters of the studio. The band stayed up for three days straight and recorded 22 new Deadëye tracks. Catering provided by Jason's outstanding restaurant. By the end of the sessions, Sonyta changed her name to Sonya.

Deadëye and recording engineer, Walt, slammed through every song's overdubs while Doc ferried the ladies to an airport somewhere. The entire record took less than a hundred hours to record and two days to mix.

With a couple of days before one of New Jersey's 66greatest rock bands was scheduled to arrive and take over the studio (that's a joke, there's no such thing as a good New Jersey rock band) Doc said, "C'mon, Princess. get that acoustic record shit done so we can get outta here."

"You were serious about that?" Deadëye asked Doc.

"My godfather said Jimmy Page fucked up by waiting too long to make a solo acoustic record."

"Jimmy Page never made an acoustic record."

"Exactly," Doc said. "You don't wanna end up like Jimmy Page."

Deadëye blasted out his five-song, solo EP in a day and a half despite the fact he did, indeed, want to end up like Jimmy Page. With the master of the acoustic EP at the vinyl-pressing plant, the artwork for the latest line of Deadëye apparel at the T-shirt factory, and the month-long solo tour of America booked, Deadëye was at a loss for shit to do for a month.

"We need a few days off," Doc said. "We're going to Montreal."

15
MONTREAL

M ONTREAL, CANADA OCCUPIES A SPECIAL PLACE in North American culture.

Walking down the street and shuffling his feet, Deadëye observed, "There's a demonic presence here, Doc."

"They hate us, 'cause they ain't us," Doc said.

Deadëye understood but wanted to know. "Why are we hanging out someplace where they hate us?"

"They hate us everywhere."

"Good answer, Doc. We're rock 'n' roll outlaws," Deadëye said. "If they don't hate us, we aren't doing our job. When we hit town, the motherfuckers better lock up their daughters."

Ever the promoter, Doc said, "Lock your daughter in the car in our secure parking lot, Deadëye drives the ladies wild."

"Lock your daughter in the car? That's a terrible idea!" Deadëye said.

Doc thought for a moment, looked Deadëye dead in the eye, and asked him, "What do you want on your pizza?"

"Here's the deal, Deadëye," Doc started. "We're around here for a month. Then we do the solo tour, then we're back in L.A. for a month, then we hit the road with the ladies."

"What the hell do we do around here for a month?" Deadëye asked.

"We take it easy. Ish. I've booked a studio for three weeks—do another solo record or do something with some of these Eurotrash electronic fuckers around here. The lead time on vinyl pressing is three months right now, so we want material in the can we have ready when we need it."

"The just-in-time Toyota manufacturing system of production?"

"That doesn't work with people in the music business," Doc explained. "Music business people are stupid. They fuck shit up a couple of times before we get what we paid for. Thus delaying our ability to own castles with moats expeditiously."

"Fuck those people, then."

"Exactly. We take no fucking prisoners. We are the hunters, not the hunted."

"That was the best pizza I've ever had in my life," Deadëye told Doc on the way out of the restaurant.

"I agree. We need tequila."

Doc led Deadëye to a hole-in-the-wall dive bar where a boisterous crowd of bikers were hazing a prospect. In the ladies room. With auto parts.

"Do we have life insurance?" Deadëye asked Doc.

"We're good. I was in prison with the dude who runs this place."

The bikers eventually left and a beautiful woman with an acoustic guitar appeared on the bar's graffiti-covered stage. The angelic creature performed to the dozen or so patrons of the bar who expressed little enthusiasm for the entertainment on stage. Doc noticed the out-to-lunch look on Deadëye's face and said, "Oh, fuck."

In Deadëye's dead mind's eye, the brilliant and captivating woman on stage sang every song directly to him. Deadëye had no idea what was happening—all of the vocals were in French.

After a half-dozen songs, the beguiling chanteuse sat down next to Deadëye and a cocktail appeared in front of her immediately, as if by magic.

Intimidated by the woman's beauty, Deadëye babbled, "Thank you for sharing your music, you're fantastic."

"You're Deadëye," the lovely lady said in a French-dipped accent. Deadëye recoiled as if struck by lightning. "I saw the video of you on the train. I love trains." Doc laughed and left—Deadëye was unaware of any train videos. "I am Charlotte. Why are you in Montreal?"

"I just finished a U.S. tour with my band and did some recording in New York. I'm here for a month then I'm doing a solo acoustic tour. Why are you in Montreal, Charlotte?"

"I'm a retired acrobat," Charlotte answered with a wry smile and a glimmer in her eyes.

"Wow," Deadëye exclaimed, "I've never met an acrobat."

"You've never met a stripper?"

She's the whole package, Deadëye thought to himself, even after Charlotte revealed her past as an acrobat was with The Cirque du Soleil, not as a stripper. After an accident or three on the aerial silks, Charlotte graduated to choreography and production design.

"When's your next show?" Deadëye asked Charlotte.

She answered, "I am here tomorrow night."

Deadëye responded with a promise to see Charlotte again the next night then got the fuck out of there before he said or did something stupid. Doc wasn't outside in front of the bar, so Deadëye stood there for a moment until Doc's familiar, booming voice bellowed, "Deadëye! Get up here!" from an upstairs window.

Down a dark alley to the back of the building and up a flight of rickety stairs Deadëye found the proprietor's office/drug den where Doc and his old pal, G, welcomed him to the party.

"Welcome to Canada, motherfucker," G said as he handed Deadëye a beer and pointed to the pile of cocaine on his desk. "Make yourself at home."

Doc, the world's second-biggest Handsome Dick Manitoba fan, said, "The party starts now."

Deadëye woke up to Doc knocking on the door of his bedroom in their penthouse suite of a hotel in Old Montreal. "Breakfast time!"

Deadëye learned the party the previous evening lasted until 7 a.m. and no casualties were reported.

"I need a guitar," Deadëye said.

At the finest French-Canadian guitar store in Quebec, Deadëye bought two big, fat acoustic guitars and a 12-string for about $20,000 Canadian. Mainly so he could seduce Charlotte when she entered his lair to "write songs together."

"When do we run out of money?" Deadëye asked Doc back in the hotel after guitar shopping.

"Never," Doc answered, with confidence. "The dollar is really strong right now. It's like everything in Canada is half price."

"Even the hookers?"

"Especially the hookers. Eyeball wants me in New York. He's working on some licensing deals. You good here by yourself?"

"Fuck you."

Deadëye insisted Doc accompany him to Charlotte's gig at the dive bar before Doc left for the airport so he wouldn't look like a pathetic loner to the French-Canadian woman of his dreams. Charlotte took the stage just as Deadëye and Doc arrived and tore through eight songs, seven of which were not performed the previous evening.

"Bonjour," Deadëye said as Charlotte joined him at the bar after her set.

"Bonjour," Charlotte replied. "Where did your friend go?"

"New York," Deadëye replied. "He's always trying to sell a piece of me."

Charlotte chuckled and stared up at the hockey game on the screen suspended above the bar. Deadëye sensed she didn't give a fuck about hockey as he wondered if Charlotte's sparkling radiance was a product of some kind of radioactive chemotherapy.

"What does *Où Étais Tu* mean?" Deadëye asked. "You played all new songs tonight except that one."

"It's a very personal song," Charlotte said. "I've only performed it two times."

"It's a beautiful song. So much emotion."

Charlotte moved her gaze from hockey to her Old Fashioned then over to Deadëye. "*Where Have You Been?*"

Frozen and melted in time and space, Deadëye mumbled something about leaving. Charlotte said, "It's Friday night. *You're* not going anywhere. Where are *we* going?"

In Montreal, Deadëye had only been to a guitar store, a pizza place, and the dive bar he was in at that moment. And his hotel. "I bought a new guitar today…"

Deadëye was head over heels in love with Charlotte and failing to contain his emotions, as usual. Like most women, Charlotte was more intuitive than Deadëye and found his internal struggle charming. "Tu es beau," she said. And, "Je te veux," elicited a look of confusion on Deadëye's face Charlotte found enchanting—she wanted Deadëye even more. Deadëye's plan to lure Charlotte into his lair backfired as Deadëye was ensnared in Charlotte's web.

With Doc out of town and a week or so before he was expected in the recording studio, Charlotte endeavored to show Deadëye the best of Montreal.

Sadly, the best of Montreal only took a couple of days to explore. Sensing Deadëye's boredom with the Montreal landscape and his raging sex addiction, Charlotte suggested an evening of acrobatics.

"Doc, you won't believe what's happening here in Montreal," Deadëye reported. "These strip clubs—"

"I know all about it," Doc replied. "Listen, the shit going down here in New York is serious. The burger company wants to put *Your Way* in an ad campaign, and—are you sitting down?"

"I'm lying down—"

"A Chinese flying car company wants to use *If It Flies* in a Super Bowl commercial."

"Do it," Deadëye said. "Let's fucking do it."

"I'll send you some documents to sign," Doc said, "we're going nuclear.

OF COURSE, CHARLOTTE HAD AN ELECTRONICA BAND— everybody in that pseudo-French town owns a synthesizer and is a DJ. Deadëye was totally down with that and spent a week writing songs in his hotel during the day and eating hallucinogenic drugs in dance clubs with Charlotte every night. With the pending studio dates looming, Deadëye asked Charlotte to join him in the studio.

"Yes, I am on holiday for two weeks after tomorrow," Charlotte said. The planets seemed to be in alignment.

Charlotte and Deadëye shared songs and selected some for a Charlotte solo album, a few for Deadëye's next solo album, and several for a Deadëye/Charlotte duo project Charlotte named Les Amoureuses.

The combination of Charlotte's voice, Deadëye's vocals, and six and twelve-string guitars in the studio Doc arranged on Le Plateau-Mont-Royal worked. By the time Charlotte's two-week holiday from the acrobatics company concluded, the pair finished 28 tracks, Doc was back in town, and Deadëye was ready to return to New York and mix the songs Les Amoureuses had recorded.

"Will you come visit me in New York?" Deadëye asked Charlotte.

"Maybe. I resigned from The Cirque du Soleil and I'm coming with you. Do Americans consider that a visit?"

"I HATE DEALING WITH COUPLES, but you guys are okay," Doc said.

"Thanks," Deadëye replied, "I think."

"When does she turn into a cunt?"

"When she's a superstar she might. I can't see it happening, though. She's too well-adjusted."

"Her music is fucking incredible," Doc said. "Do you want me to manage her?"

Deadëye looked the poutine-loving boatman directly in the eye and said, "Fuck yeah. She's opening every show on the solo tour until she explodes and then I'll probably be opening for her."

"You know as soon as she meets Magic and Sonya they'll form a girl band."

"They'll be a kick-ass band, I'm all for it.," Deadëye said.

Doc stared at the last gravy-covered French fry on his plate and said, "We're done dealing drugs."

"No, we're not. Our expenses will be $5 million by the time we're done recording, driving around America, fucking around in Vegas, then touring the world with the band."

Doc broke out a pen and started writing numbers on a napkin.

"What the fuck!" Deadëye exclaimed.

"Yep," Doc replied.

"We're gonna make more money from parking than the Super Bowl commercial?"

"Yep."

"How the hell do we make money from parking?" Deadëye asked Doc.

"Parking."

"Parking?"

"Parking. I've only booked shows where there's no parking."

"Then how do we make money from parking if there's no parking?"

"Don't worry about it."

Sure enough, Doc collected giant bags of currency in every town the Deadëye and Charlotte tour performed. Doc's managerial acumen generated ridiculous amounts of cold, hard, parking lot cash. More on that later.

"Doc, you're a motherfucking mad scientist of rock 'n' roll," Deadëye said, one day.

"I was done with rock 'n' roll," Doc said. "Until I saw that look in your eye and the clothes you wear."

16 ROAD TRIP U.S. TOUR

Doc, Charlotte, and Deadëye stumbled into West Hurley where boxes of records, cassettes, CDs, T-shirts, and Deadëye bobbleheads awaited. The first Deadëye solo roadshow had everything it needed to roll.

"We only have four days to mix all this shit," Deadëye told recording engineer, Walt.

"We're fucked," Walt answered. "We'll get it done, though."

While Walt and Deadëye mixed the second Deadëye solo album, Charlotte sat in the control room designing album covers and merchandise in a psychedelic, French-Canadian, monster movie style.

"Is there anything you can't do?" Deadëye asked Charlotte.

"Yes. For those things I have you." Deadëye wrote and recorded *For Those Things I Have You* on the spot.

Mixing 28 songs in four days happened, miraculously, then factories all over the place tasked with printing, manufacturing, assembling, and delivering the goods went to work while the Doc, Charlotte, and Deadëye show departed the Catskills headed for the first show in Boston.

Savvy music business guy, Eyeball, promoted the Deadëye solo record relentlessly and posted one Charlotte song online for streaming.

Eyeball called. Doc put him on the speaker as Deadëye piloted the sprinter van through hellish parts of Connecticut. "Something weird's going on."

"You have a date with a woman?" Deadëye asked.

"Funny," Eyeball said. "Charlotte's song is going viral on the streaming services. We need a video right now."

"Which song is streaming?" Charlotte asked.

"That way tattoo song."

"*Où Étais Tu?*" Deadëye asked.

"Yeah, that's what I said."

Doc took over. "I'll have a video for you in three days," he said, then ended the call.

"I know exactly what I want," Charlotte said.

Doc and Charlotte conferred, made phone calls, sent text messages, and planned a party.

The Boston show impressed all 25 people in attendance. Doc

and Charlotte were waiting in the van with the engine running right outside the front door of the club as Deadëye finished his last song and sprinted to the sprinter van. At 4 a.m. the tired trio strolled into a Brooklyn soundstage where breakfast, acrobatic gear, supermodels, and a robust production team almost immediately said Deadëye's favorite word—action.

While Charlotte and her circus friends cavorted on aerial silks and giant pillows, Deadëye found a place to take a nap in a conference room. In the middle of a nightmare about being lost in the catacombs of Los Angeles, a production assistant rousted Deadëye and handed him a cup of coffee. "It's time for your scene, Deadman."

Director Charlotte choreographed all of the action, taking great pleasure as a trio of her naked circus friends choked, slapped, scratched, licked, and spit on Deadëye. Then she joined in.

"Cut!" yelled the producer.

Fuck that guy, Deadëye thought to himself, out loud.

The camera crew followed Charlotte to the biker bar where the show was that night, grabbed some more footage, and then ran back to the studio to edit the video.

Most of the 40 or so bar patrons in New York who were in the room appeared to be enjoying the Charlotte show. A handful of foreign exchange student types arrived specifically to see Charlotte.

"We need her merch right away," Deadëye told Doc.

"No shit," Doc replied. "We'll have a bunch waiting for us in D.C. I've placed orders with four different T-shirt companies. We'll see shit show up at every venue and, if things really heat up, we'll have some all ready to ship wherever we need it. We might have CDs and cassettes in Nashville. The vinyl is a couple of weeks away, at least. Those record-pressing fuckers are slow."

"Eyeball thinks Charlotte is about to blow the fuck up," Deadëye said.

"Eyeball has no idea what's about to hit him. He needs help right now. We're hiring the first smart motherfucker we run into and sending them to L.A."

"I'm a smart motherfucker," said the Charlotte look-alike at the bar there to see Charlotte perform who was eavesdropping on the conversation about Charlotte. "I just finished my undergrad at NYU and I'm taking a year off before I start law school."

Fast on his feet, Doc asked the fetching young lady, "What's one good reason we should bring you in as an intern for a year?"

"I have a degree from NY fucking U—Master of Arts in Music Business with a Special Concentration in Music Technology. Motherfucker." Then the perfect job candidate took her drink, walked to the stage, and watched Charlotte murder the audience with her final song, *Où Étais Tu?*

At the close of her set, Charlotte told the audience, "Please join me for a drink at the bar, I will perform another song with Deadëye later."

"She will?" Deadëye asked Doc, who simply shrugged.

Charlotte met all of her fans and brought them all to the bar. "Doc, Deadëye, this is Pearl," Charlotte said as she introduced them to the NY fucking U graduate. "Tell Eyeball she's on her way to Los Angeles."

"I am so excited!" Pearl squealed as she grabbed Charlotte and shed real tears.

When the Charlotte fangirl situation paused for a second, Deadëye asked Charlotte, "What song are we doing together?"

"For Those Things I Have You," Charlotte answered. "Play that one last so all of the women stay. We're going to have a hit with that song."

Doc grabbed Charlotte and Pearl and found a quiet spot in the bar manager's office to talk about merch. Within two minutes Doc realized he was in the presence of two remarkably capable people who were about to make some shit happen. So he shut up while Charlotte and Pearl laid out Charlotte's marketing strategy and designed a line of apparel/accessories before Deadëye finished his first song.

"Put me on the first fucking flight in the morning to Los Angeles," Pearl said. "All I need is 15 minutes to pack and I'm off to the airport."

And so it was. Doc gave Pearl a bunch of cash, set her up with a furnished apartment across the street from the Fire Tornado Records office in West Hollywood, and booked her a first-class ticket departing at 7 a.m. And he instructed her to arrive at the airport three hours early so she could get hammered in the first-class lounge at JFK before departure. Pearl told her New York City landlord to eat shit and die, gave her cat away, and broke up with her college boyfriend via text. Charlotte ordered Pearl office furniture, computer equipment, and home furnishings. Eyeball was thrilled and ready to meet Pearl at LAX and make her feel at home.

"Don't be creepy, Eyeball," Charlotte told Eyeball.

Pearl said, "I like creepy."

"Perfect," Charlotte said.

Doc looked at his phone and announced, "We'll have the video by 3 p.m. tomorrow."

"Fuck, yeah!" Pearl exclaimed. "That's noon L.A. time, Imma hit the ground running."

Charlotte told Pearl, "Your Mac Pro will be waiting for you on your desk," then asked her, "Is there anything else you need, love?"

"Nothing," Pearl responded.

Doc said, "We're paying you $2,000 a week, leasing you an apartment and a car, and Eyeball is ordering you a company credit card. You're Chief Marketing and Technology Officer. Send everybody a press release tomorrow."

"Holy shit, if you didn't look exactly like my dad I would suck your cock right now," Pearl revealed.

"I'll put on a mask," Doc said.

"Come," Charlotte said, perhaps as a pun, "it's time for me to do it with Deadëye and I want you to watch, Pearl."

"Duet?" Doc mused.

Charlotte and Deadëye had never performed or even rehearsed *For Those Things I Have You* before, so Deadëye didn't know what to expect—he had no idea she even knew how to play the song. Charlotte picked up the 12-string, grabbed a stool, and sat down next to Deadëye as he strummed the introduction to the song. Deadëye's somewhat tentative approach to the song wasn't working for Charlotte. so she joined him and raised the musical intensity. Les Amoureuses traded verses and shared choruses in the typical duet fashion. By the end of the song all eyes were on Charlotte and the audience was mesmerized. So was Deadëye.

Charlotte collected phone numbers and Instagrams from her fans while Deadëye joined Doc at the bar. Doc told Deadëye, "We're recording the shows in D.C. and Richmond. I think we should pick up Sonyta, err, Sonya, and bring her with us to do percussion—shakers and shit—for the rest of the tour."

"Yes," Deadëye agreed.

"And we're hiring a film crew to film the show in Nashville. On actual film."

"Awesome."

"We might wanna stay in Nashville for a couple of extra days so we can throw a release party for your record, do some press for all three projects, and make some friends. We can do that if I move some dates around and we start flying instead of driving."

"Sounds great. Everything we do on this tour needs to be documented, in my opinion."

"I agree, Deadëye. Go get your girlfriend, our hotel is in Philadelphia."

As Doc snorted amphetamines and piloted the sprinter van through the hell that is New Jersey, Charlotte fell asleep in Deadëye's arms with the biggest smile on her face. She was clearly living her best life and knew nothing could stop her. Deadëye joined her in slumber and dreamt of cave elephants running a lemonade stand and speaking Spanish.

17
NASHVILLE

Shows in Philadelphia, D.C., and, the Deadëye stronghold of Richmond, Virginia, saw larger and larger audiences as Pearl's relentless promotion of Charlotte's video yielded results. Charlotte and Sonya fell in love with each other at first sight in Richmond, then the Doc/Deadëye/Charlotte/Sonya show flew to Nashville where Doc carved out a five-day stay. Eyeball, Pearl, and Magic joined the party in Tennessee, as well.

Every day in Nashville started with meetings and interviews in the morning, lunch with music business people, afternoons hanging out or performing at radio stations and/or happy hours, and then a show somewhere every single night. With videographers around a lot of the time. The warm welcome and apparent enthusiasm for the Charlotte/Deadëye crew in Nashville struck a deep chord in the whole crew.

"Fuck Vegas," Doc told Deadëye. "We're coming back here to rehearse for the tour with your band."

"Works for me," Deadëye said. "We should open an office here. Have Eyeball spend a few days a month here, Pearl spend a few days a month here, know what I mean?"

"I can get that done in five minutes," Doc said. And he did. Then he told Deadëye, "Looks like we're all going to Europe after the U.S. tour."

"I'm available."

Sonya was ebullient and maybe a little bit hammered one evening at a rooftop soiree arranged with a who's who of Nashville music industry intelligentsia.

"Deadguy, I like your little acoustic act, but, when we hit the road with the electric band we need to be heavy as fuck. Heavy as fuck."

"We will be."

"We need to be heavier. We need to murder motherfuckers with high-volume rock 'n' roll"

"Should we add another guitar player, or—"

"Yes."

"Who?"

"Have you heard Charlotte play an electric guitar?"

"Oh, God," Deadëye groaned. "Don't tell me she's a guitar hero, too."

"See those fuckers she's talking to?" Sonya asked as she gestured toward Charlotte charming a handful of the fiesta's guests. "They run Gibson and they think she's the next Taylor whatshername."

"Great!"

"When she's done talking to them, take the two guys on the right somewhere and tell them Charlotte's joining our band and you want an endorsement deal. You need eight 100-watt heads, eight four-by-twelve cabinets, two of every foot pedal they sell, and a couple of Non-Reverse Firebirds. And keep it all a secret. Have 'em send the gear to Eyeball in Los Angeles."

"Drag her away from them and I'll get it done in ten minutes," Deadëye said.

Sure enough, the executives at Gibson jumped at the opportunity to work with Charlotte, were sworn to secrecy until the end of the acoustic tour, and agreed to send a truckload of gear to Los Angeles. They also invited the Deadëye gang to their factory and offices the next day where the whole crew was given a tour and Charlotte cried when presented with an extraordinary wine red Hummingbird acoustic.

"I love Nashville," Charlotte said. "The people are so friendly."

"I know you do," Deadëye said. "We'll be back in a month."

Before the trip to Gibson, Doc and Deadëye met with Eyeball and Pearl to review.

"Every publishing company, record company, distribution company, publicity firm, and all the rest want to do business with us," Eyeball reported.

"Can we do all of that shit ourselves?" Doc asked.

"Yes," Pearl answered, emphatically. "Fuck those people. They don't understand what we're doing here."

"We're coming back to Nashville to rehearse for the electric tour. Then we're doing a residency here and a residency in Los Angeles," Doc informed the Fire Tornado team. "After the States, we're spending the summer in Europe. We need massive publicity in Europe. Do we know anyone?"

"Yes," Eyeball and Pearl answered in unison.

Doc thought for a minute and everyone could see the wheels turning in his head. "Eyeball, Pearl, I need you both in London as soon as possible. We need a presence in London all day, every day. I'll set up meetings with some people I know. Meet with everybody you can you know or you want to know, stay there as long as it takes. We need to crack London, then we need to figure out which Eastern European or Scandinavian country we want to really dominate. For fun. And so we can headline their huge football stadium every year."

"Like Manowar in Bulgaria," Deadëye said.

"Ross the motherfucking Boss," Eyeball said.

Pearl brought facts, figures, and great ideas everybody agreed to pursue.

"Don't wait for us," Doc told Pearl and Eyeball. "Just do it."

"Duet?" Deadëye asked.

Pearl's top priority was developing an e-commerce site—she was given the green light and told to get it done yesterday.

"Who's going to do the fulfillment?" Pearl asked.

Doc, remembering the night he met Pearl asked, "Are you unfulfilled?"

"Not at all," Pearl shot back. "I'm getting so much pussy."

"Save some for me," Eyeball said.

Doc spun brain wheels again and said, "We do it ourselves from here in Nashville. We need someone to keep the lights on in the office and, for now, our representative here can do the shipping. We definitely need someone in London to do that, too. If we outsource the fulfillment the fuckers will fuck everything up and we get blamed. I believe we do everything we can in-house. We're building an empire here."

"Where do we find a Nashville rep?" Eyeball asked.

Deadëye said, "They fall from the sky," just as Charlotte and Sonya joined the festivities.

Charlotte parroted Deadëye, "They fall from the sky. Deadëye, come, I need you to write me that song right now."

"In that order?" wise guy Doc wisecracked as Charlotte, Deadëye, and Sonya excused themselves to do some songwriting.

The group groaned at Doc's ribald humor, as usual, then Doc continued developing business strategy. "We need more than warm bodies in offices, we need more Eyeballs and Pearls."

"I can get an ass-kicking motherfucker straight outta NYU here tomorrow," Pearl said.

"FaceTime that ass-kicking motherfucker right now," Doc commanded.

So Pearl called her classmate from NYU, Cameron, who said, "I'm in Nashville right now."

Pearl told Cameron, "Get the fuck over here right fucking now."

While taking a break to enjoy the hotel's breakfast buffet, Doc asked, "Where's Magic?" when he realized Deadëye's bass player was missing in action.

"She met some plastic surgeon last night, he's giving her free tits today," Pearl reported. "She won't be back."

Cam, as Doc named him, arrived about the same time the disheveled trio returned from "songwriting." He impressed the crowd, was hired on the spot, and was given the keys to the Fire Tornado Nashville kingdom. Cam told the assholes at the country music company he worked for to eat shit and die and spent the next couple of days learning how crazy his new co-workers were. Pearl treated Cam like her little puppy dog, which gave Doc a sense of security.

"That was fast," Deadëye said, eliciting giggles from Charlotte and Sonya.

"He fell out of the sky," Eyeball said. Eyeball's sexual frustration was fucking up the whole room's vibe, so Sonya led him to lead her to his room. Doc stared at Pearl's pearl necklace, Pearl pretended not to notice. Things were getting weird.

Doc, Cam, Eyeball, and Pearl drove in a separate car to and from Gibson so the Fire Tornado crew could bombard Cam with an avalanche of information. Doc was impressed at Cam's note-taking skills and his well-manicured cuticles.

In the Gibson Custom Shop, Sonya broke the news to Deadëye about the loss of bass player Magic.

"Again?" Deadëye asked.

"Again," Sonya said. Then she asked, "Where do we find a new bass player?" Deadëye and Charlotte sang *They Fall from the Sky* together. Apparently, they wrote a song, too.

18 LOS ANGELES

THE DEADËYE/CHARLOTTE ACOUSTIC double-headlining bill tore through Texas, the Southwest, Vegas, Seattle, and Portland. By the time the tour reached the Pacific Northwest, shows were selling out and the crowds of young ladies in attendance stood in awe of Charlotte. A quick couple of dates in San Francisco and San Diego preceded two weeks in Los Angeles to set up Charlotte's record release.

Eyeball and Pearl were already back in Los Angeles from London. The Fire Tornado team met with Doc's old pal the first day they were in England and inked a deal for European management, publicity, merchandising, and distribution. ATM Management was ready to sign Deadëye/Charlotte to a global deal, but Doc knew better.

Deadëye asked Doc, "How did we get the Europe deal done so quickly?"

"The Charlotte videos."

"That makes sense."

"If ATM handles the European releases and tour to our liking we'll consider going global with them, in some way," Doc told Deadëye. "And only if Eyeball, Pearl, and Cam are taken care of. I'm on board with you and Charlotte as long as it takes."

"As long as it takes for what?" Deadëye asked.

"$100 million in the bank."

"Fuck. Okay, then."

"Each. And at least as much cold, hard, cash in addition to that." Doc said, then pivoted. "We need to stop by the office and show your girlfriend her new gear."

As predicted, Charlotte lost her mind and cried a million tears when Pearl turned on the lights in the Fire Tornado offices revealing eight Mesa/Boogie half-stacks, a Non-Reverse Firebird, a Non-Reverse Firebird 12-string, A Firebird V, and a Les Paul Goldtop.

"Holy shit!" Deadëye said.

"No shit," Doc said. 'Wait until they see the new video."

"What new video?"

"**H**AVE WE BEEN TO LOS ANGELES TOGETHER?"

"No, silly," Charlotte replied. "We met in Montreal and I made you want me more than anything else. I was in love with you before we even met."

"Stop," Deadëye said, "you're gonna make me cry."

"You're making dreams come true I never dared to dream," Charlotte said as Deadëye struggled to maintain his composure. "With you, Deadëye, anything is possible."

"Cut!" the director said. "And scene."

How Doc convinced that Coppola woman to produce a long-form theatrical music video for Charlotte, Deadëye would never know.

"She's going to be a movie star," Sonya, the company psychic told Deadëye. "The film fucks can't stop talking about how magical she looks on the big screen."

"What do we do?" Deadëye asked Sonya.

"We push the button and take the ride. That's all we can do. You're the luckiest man on the planet. Make her your number one priority. The minute you don't, she's gone."

"I do what I do because of the music, Sonya. You know that."

"Don't shoot the messenger. I'm telling you what any blind woman can see."

Deadëye stared at his shoes and muttered, "Yeah…"

"By the way, who's the new bass player?" Sonya asked.

"You'll meet her in Nashville," Deadëye said. "She used to be in Smashing Pumpkins."

"Which one?"

"The hot female bass player."

"There's been, like, ten of those," Sonya said.

"I guess we'll find out together."

DEADËYE WAS CONFUSED. "Why are we still in Los Angeles, again?"

Doc said, "Every day the offers from promoters get better and better. We're being offered support slots in arenas with every huge band you can imagine and headlining shows in theaters. My strategy is to wait a minute, do a few dates in Nashville, a few in Los Angeles, add in Chicago, New York, Austin, Richmond, then hit the European festivals."

"What about building a fan base in the States?" Deadëye asked.

"My advice is, we do some of that after Europe hit Japan, do some more after that. Break it up into small pieces. The last thing you want to do is spend three or four months driving around America."

"I get it now," Deadëye said. "How long before we get our own jet with a fireplace?"

"That doesn't work these days," Doc answered. "You'll look like a douchebag."

"How about we get a jet and make it look like a beat-up old plane? Like those cunts at the guitar companies relic guitars?"

Stopped in his tracks, Doc said, "That's a great idea. Nobody's ever done that before. Relic a private jet. That's brilliant."

"We have to do it," Deadëye said.

Doc said, "I know a guy."

Deadëye hated Los Angeles and had nightmares every time he fell asleep there.

"You lost the lawsuit, you owe the record company $200 million."

"It's all gone?"

"No. You retain your streaming rights."

"How much is that?"

"After my chunk and the administrative expenses, you get at least two or three hundred dollars every quarter."

"Thanks, Doc. I'm going back to school so I can be a nurse."

"Deadëye, there's no money in music. The only way we'll ever make any money doing this crazy shit is in parking. Trust me."

"Doc, I know you're right, and I respect your judgment."

"Thank you, Deadëye."

"But this isn't 1979."

"Really? Well, what fucking year is it, then?"

"Hot dogs."

"What?"

"We sell hot dogs. If we sell one hot every day we make more money than Spotify will pay us in a year."

"What if we only sell one hot dog at every show and it costs $1,000?"

"Why do you have to be such a pervert, Doc?"

"Good question," Doc replied.

DEADËYE HAD AN IDEA. "Doc, let's go bowling."

"Charles!" bartender Sandra said to Deadëye as he and Doc sidled up to the bowling alley bar for a few pre-game cocktails.

"Charles?" Doc asked.

"Yeah," Deadëye responded. "That's my real name."

"How are you so famous around here?" Doc asked Deadëye.

"I grew up near here and I used to be a junior professional bowler."

"That explains a lot," Doc said. "Listen, change of plans. We're going to rehearse in Vegas. I rented a big house with a recording studio in the middle of nowhere for a month to rehearse in and booked a couple of rooms on the Strip where we can sell drugs to hookers."

"Sounds like a plan, but I'm not doing it," Deadëye said.

"I bought a flatbed tow truck, too. We can fill that with all the drugs and drive it to Las Vegas—tow truck drivers never get harassed by cops."

"What do we do with the tow truck when we get to Vegas?" Deadëye asked.

"We drive it off a cliff and blow it up for your music video," Doc answered.

"What music video?" Deadëye asked.

"The music video where we blow up the tow truck with a double-decker bus on the back as it launches off the rim of a gravel quarry north of Vegas."

"Where are we getting a double-decker bus?"

Doc, always a few steps ahead, said, "I bought one of those, too. Then I sold it to the video production guys."

"I don't even want to know—"

Doc continued, "The video guys have a fast food chain client, so they're using the double-decker to advertise The Double Decker. One side of the bus will be painted for the burger, the other side for us."

"Jesus—"

"But wait, there's more," Doc said. "I'm working on the Deadëye Burger and getting one of your songs in their commercial."

"Perfect."

"And I sold the tow truck to the burger people. You and me pocket all of the income, Eyeball pays all of the expenses."

"Are we reporting the truck and the bus stolen so we can collect the insurance money, too?" Deadëye asked.

Doc looked around the bar to see if anyone was in earshot. "We don't talk about things like that," he said in a hushed voice. "Insurance fraud is a felony with no statute of limitations."

"I feel like we do at least one of those every day," Deadëye said as Sandra delivered beautifully-filled glasses of tequila to the pair of criminals.

"No, we're not collecting any insurance money. We bill all the expenses to the record company. We make sure Eyeball's end of the business is always struggling. That way he'll work harder."

"Do we really need to do that?" Deadëye asked Doc.

"Yes," Doc answered. "The music business is a full-contact sport. We stomp on the gas pedal, go full blast, take no prisoners, kick ass—"

"All of the clichés, in other words," Deadëye deadpanned. "Do that shit with Sonya, I'm not going to Vegas. Whatever bullshit I need to film can be CGI'd."

TWO
LIGHTNING STRIKE⚡

19 BACK IN NASHVILLE

S ONYA. Hired assassin. Killer drummer. The world's greatest wingman.

"It's your girlfriend's birthday on Saturday. You need to spend the whole day with her. Leave your phones at the hotel and forget about everything business-related. Go to brunch, make sure the restaurant knows it's her birthday. Then you spend the rest of the day and night at The Hermitage. While Charlotte's in the spa you can go to the bar and get hammered or watch another man do things to your girlfriend, whatever. Then, at dinner, you ask her to marry you."

"Whoa."

"I've arranged everything. You have an appointment with Maurice at the jewelry store around the corner in 20 minutes. I picked out the ring for you. Bring all your money. You walk in, you pay, you're done."

"I'm not sure we're ready for that."

"You stupid motherfucker. She's ready. That's all that fucking matters."

"Don't fucking tell anybody," Deadëye told Sonya, who rolled her eyes and looked at Deadëye like he was an idiot.

"Everybody knows except you. You're the beloved oblivious maniac who brought us all together. All of us want you to win. If you fail, we're all fucked."

"Fuck," Deadëye exclaimed. "I didn't plan to do that. I planned to sell drugs to strippers and play music."

Sonya explained a basic fact of life Americans are too stupid to realize. "Um, plans don't work. Life is about destiny. Random shit. People falling out of the sky. Everything worth anything happens by accident."

"What the fuck? I hire an assassin and end up with a drummer who turns out to be a guru?" Deadëye told Sonya. "I'll spend the rest of my life trying to find some way to thank you for your wisdom."

"Fuck you, Deadëye. Just give me co-writing credits on all of our shit and we're good."

Wow! That was the most evil way to steal a chunk of publishing the world has seen in the past fifteen minutes, Deadëye said to himself. Despite Sonya's shrewd maneuvering and manipulation, Deadëye knew what he needed to do. After the jeweler emptied his bank account, which he did, and then some.

At rehearsals that evening, Deadëye told the band, the cast, and the crew, without explanation, "We're taking Saturday and Sunday off. Completely. All of us. No business bullshit. At all. In fact, after this song, we're done until Monday at 7 p.m. Let's go. 1, 2, 3, 4…"

"Everyone is worried," Charlotte told Deadëye, in a very concerned manner. "We leave for the tour in two weeks and nobody knows the new songs."

"No, they're not. We can't work all day every day. I know we're having fun, riding a wave of success, and loving every minute of it, but we're human and we need to behave like humans. Not like Americans. More like Europeans. We're not an American band—Americans only get two weeks of vacation from their bullshit jobs every year. If they're lucky."

"I just want to spend time with you," Charlotte told Deadëye.

"Me too."

20 NEW ORLEANS / U.S. TOUR

WITH THREE DAYS OFF before the next band practice, Deadëye and Charlotte grabbed their go-bags, flew to New Orleans, disconnected from the outside world, and set up shop at the top of Four Seasons. For a minute. Then relocated to a more authentic, less corporate, boutique hotel in the Garden District. The collision of France and North America in New Orleans thrilled Montreal-native, Charlotte. As was her wont, Charlotte fell madly in love with the city and absorbed its essence like a sponge.

The Saturday morning brunch at the hotel restaurant saw the first tears of the trip when a brass band showed up to play *Happy Birthday* for Charlotte. Really loud. In a kick-ass, rousing, New Orleans jazz style. Deadëye remained consistently impressed by Charlotte's appreciation for all things awesome.

"Merci beaucoup," Charlotte said to Deadëye after she recovered from the excitement and emotions the brass band wrought.

Deadëye started that shit with the tears all over again when he told Charlotte, "Tu es l'amour de ma vie. Je t'aime de tout mon cœur. Je t'aimerai jusqu'à mon dernier souffle." He had obviously been practicing.

After brunch Deadëye and Charlotte joined the second line of a jazz funeral, took a steamboat cruise along the Mississippi River, then returned to the hotel and enjoyed an afternoon nap together, among other things.

Then came the most important performance of Deadëye's life. After dinner and dessert, Deadëye pulled a little box out of his pocket, got down on one knee in the middle of Commander's Palace, and lost his ability to speak. He simply presented an engagement ring to Charlotte, gasped as his vocal cords failed him, and stared at Charlotte. Looking for a signal. A sign. Of any kind.

"Charles, I can't…"

She knows my real name? Deadëye thought to himself as the sting of rejection killed his will to live and he scanned the room for sharp objects to stab himself to death with.

"I can't say no to you, Charles. You fucking weirdo. Yes! Yes! Yes!"

The tears, laughter, and other weird noises coming from Charlotte and Deadëye's table failed to faze other diners—four or five earlier proposals desensitized the room to overwhelming joy expressed by others. Les Amoureuses didn't give a fuck what anybody thought, anyway.

The restaurant's staff eventually ejected Deadëye and Charlotte. Not because they were hammered, which they were, but because Commander's Palace closes earlier than any fine-dining restaurant on the planet. So Deadëye and Charlotte teleported over to the Saturday night Bourbon Street madness.

Charlotte wasted no time dragging her fiancé into an acrobatics club where Deadëye saw, for the very first time, just how goofy women get with each other when one shows off a $200,000 engagement ring. In the V.I.P. rooms, Charlotte demanded to see how her ringed finger appeared on and in many parts of many ladies. Things were getting weird by the fourth acrobatics club, so Deadëye called an Uber and the blasted couple returned to their hotel unscathed, mostly.

So much for a lazy Louisiana Sunday. "Get up, Charles!" Charlotte commanded. "We're having brunch with Sofia!" Sofia demanded Charlotte and Deadëye join her and her family and friends in a French Quarter wine cellar for a spectacular Creole brunch, and so they did.

"Tomorrow, we need to film another music video," Sofia told Charlotte.

"Yes!" Charlotte exclaimed.

Sofia explained her vision for Charlotte's song, *Voodoo Eyes*, and both Deadëye and Charlotte were completely floored by Sofia's ideas. Deadëye texted Sonya and the bass player and told them to rehearse without him. Sonya said, "Fuck you! We're spending another couple of days in Vegas!"

"Perfect, see you fuckers Thursday in Nashville."

By the end of their day with Sofia and crew, Charlotte determined New Orleans would be where her and Deadëye's marital home would be. Sofia and her French rock star husband hooked them up with a rehearsal studio and a place to live, Doc re-routed Sonya and the bass player to Louisiana and arranged for Cam to drive the band's gear down from Nashville. With Deadëye and Charlotte, anything was possible.

Sonya and bass player Maria arrived in Louisiana from Vegas as Cam was adding the finishing touches to the New Orleans rehearsal space. Sonya exclaimed, "Fuck, yeah!" when she saw the magnificent 18th-century armory converted into a rock 'n' roll palace. Sonya adjusted her kit, Maria tuned her Rickenbacker, and the two of them ran through the entire set as amps sizzled and walls rattled. Sonya and Maria were determined to be the greatest rhythm section on the planet and they rehearsed all day, every day as Charlotte and Deadëye completed the *Voodoo Eyes* video shoot with Sofia.

Doc asked Cam, "Do you want to move to New Orleans?"

Cam struggled to catch his breath after moving thousands of pounds of gear up a flight of stairs—New

Orleans was the last American city to get elevators, apparently. "I brought all my stuff and everything in the office." And so it was. Goodbye, Nashville, home of nothing all that great.

T HE FULL DEADËYE ELECTRIC BAND had five days to rehearse before Nashville, Los Angeles, and a few other places in America were treated to the wild scene the three-ring circus would bring to their towns. While in rehearsals, the Charlotte solo acoustic record landed in stores and on the streaming services at the same time the Sofia long-form video for *Anything is Possible* emerged.

Sofia showed up at rehearsals one day and stood in a paralytic manner in the doorway as the heaviest band in America destroyed. "Holy fuck," she said as the song ended, "That was epic. I need cameras right now." Sofia followed the band to Nashville and Los Angeles then bid a tearful goodbye as she returned to New York.

Two weeks after the release of Charlotte's album, the Deadëye electric album, *Deadëye*, landed along with an animated video of the first single, *Driver*. Doc's concept of a double-decker bus on a tow truck was replaced with a supersonic double-decker bus flying through time and space with Deadëye driving. The band left Los Angeles for three weeks of theater shows ending in New Orleans and, after that, a couple of weeks off to regroup.

21 LONDON CALLING

ODDLY, THE LONDON MUSIC SCENE greeted Deadëye more enthusiastically than Charlotte. Doc expressed his displeasure with the cast of characters running the show at ATM and threatened to spend all day, every day, in their offices until Charlotte was a household name in the United Kingdom.

"After our European run, we're coming back here for one, triumphant show," Doc said. "Make it fucking happen! We've worked too hard to have you fucking limeys fuck everything up!"

The British Isles tour hit London, Manchester, Birmingham, Glasgow and Dublin. The punters were skeptical as the Charlotte/Deadëye acoustic opening act started the shows. When the heaviest band on the planet hit the stage with ferocious rock 'n' roll power, all doubts were extinguished.

Shows in Copenhagen, Stockholm, Berlin, Barcelona, Madrid, and Paris had the desired effect on the continent. After the last show in Paris, the band had three weeks off before one show in London. Sonya and Maria went on a whirlwind trip around Eastern Europe while Deadëye and Charlotte regrouped in Paris and wrote songs together.

"My new video!" Charlotte screamed.

Sure enough, Fire Tornado dropped the *Voodoo Eyes* video unexpectedly one day, to great acclaim, and, finally, London figured Charlotte out.

Doc called. "Everything is blowing the fuck up in the U.K. We're doing two nights in London, now, before Japan and Australia."

"What's after that?" Deadëye asked.

"The summer festivals in Europe," Doc said.

"Great," Deadëye said. "We'll do London, Japan, Australia, Europe, then we need a break."

"A break? What about America?"

"America can wait. Charlotte's making a movie," Deadëye said. "Sofia's people will be calling you to work out the details of the contract. Make sure I get a small part."

"Anything else?" Doc asked.

"Are we ready to tell him?" Deadëye asked Charlotte.

"He doesn't know?" Charlotte asked.

"No, nobody knows," Deadëye said.

"Fuck you," Doc said. "I know everything."
"Okay, then. Bye, Doc!"
"Wait!"
"Doc, can we do one show in Montreal after Europe?" Charlotte asked.
"Yes. That's what I didn't know?"
Charlotte blurted out, "We're getting married in New Orleans!" and ended the call.

In their three weeks in Paris, Charlotte and Deadëye wrote six songs for another Deadëye rock band record and eight songs for a non-acoustic Charlotte solo album. For fun, they also wrote a Christmas song, booked a day in a studio, and knocked that one out.

All Deadëye and Charlotte wanted to do was return to New Orleans and build a life together in Louisiana. Charlotte and her sister, Juliette, spoke for hours on the phone every day planning the wedding. While Charlotte and Deadëye toured the world, Juliette visited New Orleans to scope out event venues, audition brass bands, and who knows what else.

Doc hired promoters in Japan and Australia who sent Japanese and Australian press to see the shows in London, interview the band, and fall asleep in Soho doorways where policemen knew their names. Good times.

Charlotte's bestie and a crew from the circus company flew in from Montreal to handle production design and lighting for the London shows. Doc hired Sofia's recommended film crew to capture the shows on film for future release. Deadëye, Charlotte, Sonya, and Maria reconnected for a couple of days of rehearsal, pre-production, and press, then destroyed London with Deadëye's rock 'n' roll power. The band was energized and on fire after their break and took that momentum through Japan, Australia, and beyond Charlotte's emotional return to Montreal.

Before the big show in Montreal, Deadëye and Charlotte visited the dive bar where they met, played a short set of songs together, and thanked the proprietor in every way they could for bringing them together.

Doc said, "We have an offer from Japan for a second tour with a massive guarantee."

"We're not ready to commit to that, Doc. Release the London shit, the *Live in Japan* album, the Montreal show, slowly, over time. My other solo shit. Whatever," Deadëye told Doc. "We're doing the wedding in six weeks, the honeymoon for three weeks, then the movie for three months. How much fucking content do we need?"

"The record company needs more to do," Doc said.

Deadëye asked Doc, "Have you heard Sonya sing and play guitar?"

"No. What?"

"Make a record with Sonya."

"Jesus…"

"And tell Eyeball and Pearl to get out there and find some new talent."

"They don't know how to do that. I know how to do that. You know how to do that. The only other person I know of who can do that…"

"Who?"

"Sonya."

"Damn, you're right," Deadëye said. "She probably knows ten great bands in Phnom Penh you can choose from.

Two weeks into their pre-wedding vacation, Deadëye and Charlotte hit the rehearsal studio and fired up their giant stacks of amplifiers. They brought in a death metal drummer, a jazz-fusion bassist, and a mutant synthesizer wizard. All from Craigslist. The new band worked out the songs from the Paris writing sessions and wrote a few new ones. Then recorded everything live using a mobile recording unit in a taco truck parked just outside. While the truck was there, Deadëye and Charlotte recorded twenty or so acoustic songs, as well.

"Doc we made a new record," Deadëye told his manager.
"What? When?"
"We got bored. We have a bunch of electric shit and a shitload of acoustic songs. And tons of video. I'll send it to you."
"Awesome. I'll be in N'awlins a few days before the wedding in case you need anything."
"Drugs."
"Like I said…"

22
WEDDING

JULIETTE ARRIVED IN NEW ORLEANS two weeks before the wedding to help Charlotte be the best bridezilla possible.

As Deadëye stared in disbelief at Juliette's incredible beauty, Charlotte told him, "I am the ugly one." Thus giving birth to another hit, *I Am the Ugly One*.

Deadëye remembered meeting Charlotte's sisters and parents in Montreal but failed to appreciate their inner and outer beauty that evening in Canada. Since Deadëye's family were all dead, ironically, Deadëye relied on Doc to fill the seats on his side of the aisle at the wedding. The band members, the record company people, the U.K. operation, friends from Japan and Australia, and at least a handful of hookers and reporters attended the ceremony. Sofia's posse, Charlotte's family and friends from Canada, and new friends from New Orleans, Nashville, and other places rounded out the party. And it was a party. A multi-day monster of a party.

"My last coupla weddings weren't this long," Deadëye told Doc.

"No shit. When the fuck does this end?"

Doc knew. The Canadians, the Fire Tornado crew, and the foreign press contingent arrived in time for the Friday evening festivities at the jazz place. Then there was the Saturday riverboat booze cruise, rehearsal dinner, and the coed acrobatic excursion. Then the wedding on Sunday. Then the reception. Then Deadëye and Charlotte removed themselves from their favorite New Orleans dive bar to an undisclosed location as everyone at the reception continued to get hammered and laugh about Deadëye's real name.

Deadëye and Charlotte spent their first moments alone as a married couple at, of all places, The Four Seasons. In a big, silly, ridiculous hotel suite bigger than most houses in New Orleans. Once the marriage was consummated a couple of times in each room, Deadëye and Charlotte invited their craziest friends over and the party went nuclear. Eyeball did his fire-breathing act for the wedding ceremony hookers. Pearl showed the foreign press what a party shower was all about. Doc calculated damages for the U.K. operation to pay. Cam ordered room service to do things not typically included on the room service menu. Sonya and Maria kidnapped Charlotte's sisters, who pretended to be horrified as they were baptized.

Thanks to Doc's friends in the pharmaceutical industry, Deadëye and Charlotte were alert and functional enough to climb over the party's wreckage and out the door to the airport shuttle before their friends realized what was happening. Thirty minutes later the newlyweds were in the airport lounge on the way to their honeymoon destination.

"Where are we going?" Deadëye asked Charlotte, who had done all of the wedding work.

"Mr. and Mrs. King are spending two weeks in the south of France," Charlotte said, causing Deadëye Charles to spit champagne all over the silly airport carpet.

"Are you happy with your new surname?" Deadëye asked Charlotte.

"I am happy in every way a woman could ever imagine," Charlotte answered as she grabbed Deadëye and held him tight. "You motherfucker."

Flying high above the Atlantic, Deadëye and Charlotte needed to know their friends and family were okay after the seriously fucked-up shit they started at the after-party.

Doc reported the U.K. fucks were hesitant to cover significant damages to furnishings, fixtures, and flooring in the suite, so he hung one off the balcony by his ankles for a minute, old-school style. Sonya later reported the funniest part was when Doc screamed, "And the room service bill!"

Eyeball apologized for things he didn't even do.

Cam reported he's no longer welcome at any of the Four Seasons properties worldwide.

Pearl asked that we check PornHub to see if her videos with the international press were still online—she'd requested their removal after her mom called.

Sonya and Maria were still too busy taking turns on Charlotte's sisters to respond to Deadëye's messages. Other than the occasional video clip, which Charlotte found to be hilarious. Charlotte knew her sisters were in good hands with members of the Deadëye band.

"Did you really mean it?" Charlotte asked Deadëye.

"What?"

"'Til death do us part?'"

"I didn't say that."

And that's when Deadëye learned about Charlotte's childhood all-star hockey career and her cross-checking ability.

"We can make jokes about everything in life except our love for each other and our music, Charles."

"I wasn't joking."

And that's when Deadëye learned Charlotte knew kung fu.

"You're a very lucky man, Charles King," Charlotte King said. "You're lucky we're not alone or I would show you more than kung fu."

"What, like Tai Chi?"

Lucky for Deadëye, Juliette interrupted Charlotte's mile-high martial arts display with a FaceTime call.

"Oh my God. What is happening there?" Charlotte asked as she and Deadëye attempted to ascertain the nature of the action happening on the iPhone screen.

Juliette stopped laughing and caught her breath just long enough to say, "Gangbang!"

"Juliette! Get out of there!" Charlotte said.

"It's Pearl!" Juliette screamed before she started howling with laughter as different hotel personnel manned their positions in what appeared to be a well-rehearsed routine.

"Juliette, get your sister and get the fuck out of there right now!"

Juliette said, "Colette is locked in the bedroom with Sonya and Maria. They're giving her music lessons," before she started screaming and laughing at the same time.

Deadëye whispered to Mrs. King, "Tell your sister to give the phone to Pearl."

"No! You saw Pearl! Her hands are full and she can't talk right now!"

Juliette panned around the room where Doc was visible handing the foreign press people cash out of a briefcase—hush money, presumably. Cam appeared to be barricading the door to the suite, oblivious to the fact there were two entrances. The camera captured Eyeball smoking a cigar and pounding flaming Dr. Peppers with hookers. Because he couldn't help it, Deadëye sent Doc a text recommending a pay increase for Pearl.

"Doc just sent me a text," Deadëye told Charlotte.

"Oh no…"

"He's booked another night in the suite. He says, 'This is the stuff of rock 'n' roll legend,' and there's a video clip I'm afraid to watch."

Charlotte thought for a moment and, with a wry smile, told Deadëye, "Some things I have saved my whole life. My entire life. Very special things. For my husband."

"Tai Chi?"

"Tai Chi anal."

"Whoa, that's gotta be really weird."

"How are your sisters?" Deadëye asked his new bride somewhere in France.

"We won't be hearing from them for a while."

"Why not? Are they okay?"

"Sonya ordered the *Transparent Realistic Animal Dog Dildo Knot Anal Plug Butt Plug Big Giant Monster Cock Dick Suction Cup Sex Toys For Men Women* on AliExpress.com and they've all been locked in the hotel room since we left New Orleans."

"The *Transparent Realistic Animal Dog Dildo Knot Anal Plug Butt Plug Big Giant Monster Cock Dick Suction Cup Sex Toys For Men Women?*" Deadëye asked. "Not the *Transparent Realistic Animal Dog Dildo Knot Anal Plug Butt Plug Big Giant Monster Cock Dick Suction Cup Sex Toys For Men Women!*"

"Yeah, the *Transparent Realistic Animal Dog Dildo Knot Anal Plug Butt Plug Big Giant Monster Cock Dick Suction Cup Sex Toys For Men Women*," Charlotte said. "We haven't opened any of our wedding gifts, yet, by the way. The box from Sonya and Maria weighs 40 kilos, I'm told."

"Can we pretend we never received it?"

"I tried," Charlotte answered. "They called the resort in France and confirmed receipt of the package."

"What do you think's in the box?"

"At least a couple of Big Giant Monster Cocks."

"What about the other 39 kilos?"

"More cocks. French customs X-rayed the package and concluded the box—the crate, actually—contains 100 pounds of cocks."

"Is it some kind of joke gift?"

"Oh, no, not at all. We're expected to use all of the cocks—they're not Fender tweed amps collecting dust and waiting for another fire at Joe Bonamassa's house."

"Do you think Joe Bonamassa collects cocks like he collects guitars and amps?"

"No comment. That weekend trip to Los Angeles with the high school marching band for the Rose Parade damaged me permanently."

"What does Joe Bonamassa have to do with that?"

"He told me he was the Grand Marshall and I was under arrest. Then he tied me down on top of all that tweed with those curly guitar cables."

"Which color cables?"

"The neon ones."

"What a pervert."

"Yeah, and then his mom came over. And things got weird. They made me watch."

"Dear God! That man is a monster!"

"Don't worry. I took a shit in one of the open-backed combo amps. He'll never find it."

"That fucker has Tommy Bolin's Les Paul."

"He also has a prolapsed rectum after that post-Rose Bowl party. Who knew he was such a Longhorns fan?"

"Well, anybody into tweed that much…"

"How long do you expect our marriage to last, Charlotte?"

"Like the car chase scene in The Blues Brothers, we never want it to end."

"The one at the end of the film or the one through the shopping mall?"

"Yes, Charles."

"Good answer, Mrs. King."

"If you ever leave me I will hunt you down, duct tape you to a giant cactus in the middle of the desert, and murder you. Slowly. With an axe. And one of those Tesla flamethrowers."

"Those bootleg, so-called, flamethrowers are, basically, roofing torches encased within a plastic box designed to appeal to morons with extremely poor taste in product design."

"Elon is a weirdo. Anyway, you'll die with one of his *Transparent Realistic Animal Dog Dildo Knot Anal Plug Butt Plug Big Giant Monster Cock Dick Suction Cup Sex Toys For Men Women* shoved up your ass and held in place by another *Transparent Realistic Animal Dog Dildo Knot Anal Plug Butt Plug Big Giant Monster Cock Dick Suction Cup Sex Toys For Men Women*. Your cries for help will be stifled by the *Transparent Realistic Animal Dog Dildo Knot Anal Plug Butt Plug Big Giant Monster Cock Dick Suction Cup Sex Toys For Men Women* shoved down your throat."

23 MOVIE STAR

MOVIE-MAKING LOOKS FUN ON THE OUTSIDE.
"Do I really need to be here?" Deadëye asked Sofia halfway through day two of the planned 40-day shoot.

"Motherfucker, you stay. Charlotte needs you now more than ever. This acting bullshit is fucking brutal. Forget all of your bullshit. Listen to what Charlotte says. Be present. Comfort her. The film business eats people alive. Every. Single. Time."

"No one here gets out alive?"

"Fuck. You're now assistant director, that means you need to be on the set every day, If you fuck up, you'll never work in this town again."

"Oh no! What will I do if I can never work in Baton Rouge again?"

"Let me put it in simple terms a dumbfuck like you can understand," Sofia said. "I can convince your wife to get rid of you in five minutes. Understand?"

"You're not that evil."

"Yes she is," Charlotte said as she walked into the part of the trailer that pops out to make a larger yet still uncomfortable dining area. "I overheard your entire conversation. Sofia, you're not evil. You're an evil cunt. You're an evil fucking cunt."

"Charlotte, this business is tough and—"

"And you're a fucking cunt. Fuck you. Get the fuck out of my trailer. You fucking cunt."

Sofia vacated the recreational vehicle, and Charlotte laid across Deadëye's lap and began to cry. For a few seconds until she started laughing hysterically.

"My contract is guaranteed!" Charlotte said. "I get paid no matter what!"

And that's when Deadëye and Charlotte bought Doc a new boat. Nobody knows how Doc convinced the studio to execute a contract requiring the production company to pay Charlotte her entire fee plus points on the deal given she showed up and worked more than one day on the set.

"We rock 'n' roll all night and party every day," Charlotte announced as she gathered her belongings and grabbed a pulled-pork sandwich from the craft services table on her way out of the film's base camp and back into the real world.

"That was an epic scene," Deadëye told Charlotte in the car on their way back to New Orleans.

"Do you think I was acting?" Charlotte asked her husband.

"Maybe," Deadëye answered. "But it doesn't matter. I know you're not acting when you're playing a Non-Reverse Firebird through 400 watts off musical power and 16 Celestions."

24 MORE IS BETTER

Doc called and Deadëye put him on the speaker. "Charlotte, did you really quit the film on the second day of shooting?"

"I didn't want to. I was forced to," Charlotte said. "Sofia threatened to destroy my family. Charles saved me. And he saved our family."

"And your contract saved us about six months," Deadëye added. "What's fucking next?"

"Go rehearse and write songs. I'll be busy dealing with all of the studio's damage control people and negotiating

Charlotte's settlement for a few days. I already have at least 20 messages from those fucks. Turn off your phones and go radio silent. They'll pay us extra to shut the fuck up, so don't talk to anybody about anything."

"Where are Sonya and Maria?" Charlotte asked. "We need them now."

"They're here, I'll put 'em on a plane."

"Where's here?" Deadëye asked.

"Montreal. You don't really want to know any more than that," Doc said. "Call me if you need anything from Canada."

Deadëye said, "Tell the fuckers at Gibson we need Flying V's, SGs, and Explorers."

"And a Firebird bass!" Charlotte added.

"And more amps," Deadëye added. "Deadëye is about to go nuclear!"

As if by magic, within three days the reconvened Deadëye band had a truckload of new gear from Gibson plus an entourage of foreign press and paparazzi hanging around to see what kind of craziness might happen.

Sonya brought up the elephant in the room. "Pearl turned the Los Angeles office into an underground gangbang club."

"What does that mean?" Deadëye asked.

"It's a club run by a woman where women can go to get gangbanged in a safe environment," Sonya said.

"Has that affected her work performance at Fire Tornado?" Deadëye asked.

"I don't think so," Sonya answered. "If anything it's boosted her self-esteem and she's getting a lot more cardio in."

Charlotte stood uncharacteristically speechless. Sonya asked her, "Do you have a question, Charlotte?"

"Uh—how safe is this gangbang club environment? I hate going to the gym."

Deadëye shifted the band's gears and pointed to the other elephant in the room—the giant stack of boxes. "New gear."

Maria, Sonya, and Charlotte devoured cardboard with a ferocity not seen since Pearl's last visit to Montreal.

Maria discovered a Firebird bass, four 800-watt Mesa/Boogie bass heads, and four four-by-ten cabinets.

The massive pile of DW drums and Zildjian cymbals plus the assorted hardware and associated drum bullshit thrilled Sonya and occupied her for a dozen hours.

Deadëye and Charlotte unboxed Flying V after Explorer after SG after Firebird plus some semi-hollow body Foo Fighters-type shit that went straight onto Reverb.

Deadëye ordered Maria a super-cool, Retro 1970s Music Man StingRay bass. And he ordered Charlotte a Music Man St. Vincent which he hid within her stack of Gibson boxes. As soon as Charlotte saw the St. Vincent she gasped, gave Deadëye a knowing glance, and ran away with it. As if she were rescuing a puppy from a mountain lion.

By the next day, the band was ready to rock with the new gear and the special packages of stimulants and hallucinogens someone hid inside the guitar cases.

"Doc, we need to hit that $100 million number as soon as possible," Deadëye said. "We can't wander all over the place like the Grateful fucking Dead forever."

"Check your email," Doc said.

Deadëye opened the email from Doc and opened the attachment.

"Really?"

"Really."

"Headlining?"

"Headlining."

"PinkPop?"

"PinkPop."

"How the fuck did that happen?" Deadëye asked Doc.

"Pearl."

"Pearl?"

"Remember that gangbang…"

"Holy shit. Don't tell anybody in the band. They're gonna lose their shit."

"Nobody knows for 48 hours," Doc said.

"The whole band'll be so fucking stoked. Fuck it, I'm telling them now."

"We're on fire, Deadëye. We'll hit a hundred mil and then some. Relax, take in all the scenery, enjoy the ride. I mean that. This is the shit. It doesn't happen twice. As much as you wanna feel like you're suffering, and you will, a little bit, when that happens, reboot your brain and recognize how fucking lucky you are. We have a great team. I got your back. Charlotte is smarter than everybody we know combined. Sonya will murder anybody who gets in our way."

"Thanks, man," Deadëye told Doc. "I get it. I needed that. Thanks."

"What's wrong, Deadëye?" Maria asked herself as Deadëye entered the rehearsal studio after his conversation with Doc.

Deadëye told Maria, "Please find Sonya and Charlotte. We need to have a band meeting at the Wolf. I'll see you there."

The band knew shit was serious when Deadëye called a band meeting across the street from the studio at The Howlin' Wolf. Because Howlin' Wolf is the ultimate motherfucker for people like Deadëye. Howlin' Wolf's legacy shall be celebrated and no bullshit shall be tolerated within the walls of any establishment named The Howlin' Wolf.

The ladies in the band scrambled into the room and sat down at the bar next to Deadëye. Doc's words earlier in the day struck a deep chord within Deadëye, so he was unable to fuck with the three spectacularly-talented women who surrounded him. "We're headlining the Saturday night at PinkPop in June."

"PinkPop? That's the greatest festival in Europe!" Maria said, and she knew.

"No fucking way!" Sonya said.

"Way," Deadëye said. "Doc just sent me the contract, I signed it. Are we ready for this shit?"

"We need more amps," Charlotte said. "Like Michael Schenker."

"Like Judas Priest," Sonya said.

"Almost all of those Marshall cabinets Judas Priest had on stage were empty," Deadëye said.

"That's a lie, Deadëye, and the singer is not gay."

"I don't give a fuck about that part. And I don't give a fuck if the cabinets were empty—that shit looked cool as fuck. The fact of the matter is, we're invading Europe, we are a team, nothing stands between us and rock 'n' roll glory this summer."

"We are one," Maria said.

Charlotte couldn't help herself, "That's what you told my sisters."

Sonya looked at Deadëye, Deadëye shrugged and said, "That's what she said."

The band, more united and solidified than ever, fortified themselves with alcohol and various powders. When the stars aligned, Deadëye, the band, staggered across the street, stumbled up the stairs, and ran through a majestic 20-song set of bone-crushing heavy rock 'n' roll.

"Perfect," Deadëye said. "We are ready to rock."

25
EUROPA

Doc refused to schedule a show before PinkPop. No warm-up shows, no club shows, nothing. So, when the band took the stage in front of a huge chunk of the 60,000 people at the festival that Saturday night, blinded by the lights, Deadëye and crew were scared shitless. Until the first chorus of the first song when thousands of crazy fuckers screamed along to the chorus:

She's the one — Pearl!
Number one — Pearl!

She got it done — Pearl!
She's the one!

Charlotte's brilliant idea to dress the band in pearl-colored clothing, play pearl-colored instruments through pearl-colored amps on a pearl stage with a pearlescent backdrop and pearl-ish lighting design must have made an impression on Pearl. Until the second song. When the entire theme of the show changed to Eyeball. After the third song, when the band destroyed all eyeballs as Charlotte took over lead vocals and murdered every motherfucker in the crowd, the band settled into its psychedelic stripes motif and dug deep into the world of heavy fucking rock 'n' roll for an hour. The ebb and flow of the world's best rhythm section plus the twin guitar and vocal attack of Charlotte and Deadëye drove a spike into the end of PinkPop Saturday like a motherfucker.

The band couldn't believe what they had just done. The Fire Tornado posse could not comprehend what they had seen with their own eyeballs. The U.K. operation knew what was coming and strutted into the festival office with that, "I told you so," swagger. Doc was stunned into speechlessness for a few minutes after the band finished.

Cam broke the tension in the camp. "All of the merch sold."

Doc woke up. "All of it?"

"All of it."

"We sold 600 pearl necklaces for $600 each?"

"Yep."

"All of the pearlescent tracksuits?"

"Yep, Imma need some help carrying all the cash to the truck."

"Are those U.K. cunts calling every motherfucker who makes yoga pants and baby-doll tees they know right now?"

"Yep. And they're begging. Begging hard."

Doc looked at Deadëye and said, "Fuck these U.K. cunts. It's time to call Tokyo."

"They already called," Deadëye said. "Every five minutes after the first song until four minutes ago. We wait for them to call, we ask them, 'Who the fuck is this, why do you keep calling, what the fuck do you want?' And then we tell them we might sign with their giant mafia business if they send us everything on our wishlist before Stockholm."

"That's a great idea," Doc said.

"Take my phone, I have tits to autograph."

While Deadëye was doing business bullshit, his wife and the rhythm section were locked inside the band's trailer backstage overcome with emotion. Deadëye opened the door, saw the trauma inside, and quietly closed it. Once he found a case of champagne, Deadëye returned to the trailer, opened the door, proclaimed victory on behalf of the entire band and the people of the United States of America, Canada, and Cambodia, then popped the first bottle of well-disturbed bubbly. Corks and cave-fermented alcohol filled the air as Charlotte, Sonya, and Maria made quick work of the first case. Doc kept the cases of bubbles coming until the PinkPop people turned the lights out and prepared to decontaminate the Deadëye trailer for the Sunday headliners, Orange County, California's own, The Offspring. Fuck Orange County and fuck The Offspring, say all people gifted with a hint of intelligence and an ounce of critical thinking ability.

Deadëye gathered his beautiful wife, then manager Doc led rock 'n' roll's newest power couple to a massive helicopter bound for Berlin where the European music and entertainment press were waiting to tear Deadëye and Charlotte apart. Cam and the rest of the band and crew jumped on a tour bus headed through Scandinavia to the next festival in Stockholm.

"Fuck 'em," Deadëye told Charlotte. "Fuck 'em."

"They hate us 'cause they ain't us?" the worn and torn comedienne asked Deadëye.

Doc finished his phone call and announced, "We'll see shipments of merch and vinyl from Japan in Stockholm on Thursday and Friday. Berlin before we get there. Then multiple shipments to Barcelona, Madrid, Paris, and London."

"Awesome. What're we doing tomorrow?" Deadëye asked Doc.

"You two lovebirds get to fuck with the worldwide music press sharks who live and breathe to knock you off your pedestal."

"We just fucking proved we're the greatest fucking rock 'n' roll band on the planet three fucking hours ago!" Deadëye said.

"That was yesterday," Doc said. "That was yesterday."

"They hate us 'cause they ain't us," Charlotte said.

"Do we have drugs in Berlin?" Deadëye asked.

Doc answered, "Yeah, I have a map."

"A map?"

"Yes, a map," Doc explained. "Our drug guy hid drugs all over town and he sent me a map of where we'll find the shit."

"What?"

"Sometimes he tapes the shit under a bus bench, other times it's under a bar. Sometimes it's behind a book in the library or a bookstore. Hidden in the pocket of a jacket nobody in their right mind would ever buy in a haberdashery. The zoo. Under rocks. In train stations."

"Very clever. I get it, now."

"I knew you would. We need to stop by the Holocaust Memorial on the way to the hotel."

IN BERLIN, THE LOVE OF DEADËYE'S LIFE became the face of the band as far as the worldwide music press was concerned. And as the woman who adopted, "They hate us 'cause they ain't us," as her catchphrase. Charlotte could do no wrong, in any language.

While the rest of the band and its traveling companions partied their way through Germany, Denmark, and Sweden, Deadëye, Charlotte and Doc fought the righteous battle against the corporate music business bastards.

A self-described influential Polish music blogger quoted Deadëye as saying, "It's life or death and we're in it to win it, motherfucker."

As the Deadëye tour bus arrived in Stockholm, Charlotte's face was on the front of the most popular Swedish magazine. Not just the most popular music magazine in Sweden, but *the* most popular magazine in Sweden. Period. Charlotte's quote on the front cover, "Pearl is the color of cum," created somewhat of a scandal in Sweden and far beyond its epicenter near Malmö. When Doc saw the image of the magazine's cover Sonya sent him, Doc howled, screamed, and ordered a shitload more merch from Japan.

"Deadëye," Doc started, "the best thing we can do now is go radio silent."

"Really? We couldn't possibly be more controversial right now?"

"Exactly. There's nothing better we can say. We shut up and make the fuckers beg for it. Anything we say right now will only diminish the power of the cum quote."

"We can't have that!" Deadëye said.

Charlotte walked into the room and said, "We can't have that. Come, Charles, we need to write that song now. *We Can't Have That.*"

"Doc, you're a genius, when the music press cunts ask for a quote, you tell them—"

"We can't have that. Jesus fucking Christ..."

Doc alerted the posse in Sweden, the offices in London, and the losers in Los Angeles to refrain from all conversation about Deadëye, Charlotte, and seminal fluid.

"Sofia keeps calling, Charles," Charlotte moaned after their songwriting session climaxed. "I miss her terribly."

"I do too. Except for the part where she said, 'I can convince your wife to get rid of you in five minutes.' Up until then, I didn't know she was such an evil cunt."

"I don't want to sound like a self-absorbed cunt, but this rocket ride to superstardom is going to fuck me up, Charles. I need female friends who know what it's like."

"Let's call Sofia, then," Deadëye said. "I'm secure enough in our relationship to give her a second chance. If you ever choose to let other people come between us it's because that's your choice. Right?"

"No. That's not right. It will be because you're an asshole. I waited my whole life for you."

"Me too. Let's find out what that cunt wants. If nothing else she'll give us some great material."

"DOC, SOFIA IS BEGGING CHARLOTTE to come back and finish the movie."

"Believe me, Deadëye, there's no way I'll be the one to leak that juicy tidbit to the *New York Post*."

"What do we do? Charlotte misses Sofia terribly. She'll never know another famous person who was there for her before she was famous."

"Well, the check cleared for the day-and-a-half she worked for Sofia last time. Don't check your bank account, you'll want to stop working the rest of your life."

"Thanks for that tip."

"I'll make it happen if that's what you and Charlotte want," Doc said. "I'm the big, bad, mean, manager motherfucker. When we can fit it in the schedule and the money is astronomical the deal will be done."

"Great."

"Remember when I told you the price was going up every day?"

"Yes, I do."

"Was I right?"

"Yes, you were."

"We haven't even fucking started, yet, Deadëye. 'Pearl is the color of cum!' You have no idea how wealthy you two are about to be."

"We're both scared to death."

"That's normal when you're a fucking astronaut. Sonya told you what to do. Push the button, take the ride."

"Are we ready to leave for Sweden, we both miss the posse?"

"Yeah, fuck this place. I'll meet you in the bar in two hours."

26
SVERIGE

LIKE CLOCKWORK, DOC ARRIVED IN THE LOBBY, said, "Off we go!" and the Doc/Charlotte/Deadëye banditos were in Stockholm in time for dinner with their favorite people on the planet.

"Some creep at McDonald's wanted to buy my underwear today," Sonya said.

"I got fingered on the subway," Maria said, "by Sonya."

Charlotte said, "Pearl is the color—"

"No!" cried everybody Deadëye and Charlotte knew in Sweden.

"—of cum," Charlotte finished and then laughed like a hyena.

Deadëye told Sonya, "You have to admit, there's nothing funnier than going on tour with a band starting at zero that becomes the biggest fucking rock 'n' roll band in the world by the second date of the tour. It's epic and awesome and we need to have fun."

"Pearl is the color of cum," Charlotte said.

"We need Eyeball and Pearl here, Doc. Can we do that?"

"Yes, I'll make it happen."

"Should we invite Sofia?"

"Yes," Doc said. "If she really wants Charlotte, she'll be here."

"Thanks, Doc."

"My advice, when, not if, she shows up, is to be yourself. You don't need to be a dick, you don't need to be fake. She fucked up, we all fuck up, no need to rub her face in the $25 million it will end up costing her."

"$25 million?"

"Domestically. Probably twice that from the overseas box office and $1 million every year as long as you live."

"Holy shit!"

"Then there's the song placements I'm negotiating. That's a few hundred thousand every year for a few years, at least."

"Sofia texted, she'll be here tomorrow. What should I do?" Charlotte asked Doc and Deadëye.

"Whatever you're comfortable doing," Deadëye said, "She's—"

"I'm not comfortable with any of this shit! I don't know what the fuck to do! I need help!"

Doc stepped up at just the right time. "Tomorrow, we're all going to the Abba Museum, then the Avicii Experience, and then I've booked us a private room at a great restaurant for dinner. Tell Sofia you can't wait to see her and her posse tomorrow night."

"Eyeball and Pearl are on the way," Deadëye reported, "they'll be here tomorrow afternoon."

"Charles, when do you expect us to have a normal life?"

"Here's the deal, beautiful. Tell me what you want and when you want it. I will make it happen."

"Do you mean that?"

"Yes," Deadëye answered. "We're good. We're successful. We've made it. We don't need anything from anybody. We're doing this to have fun with our friends and create amazing memories together. Doc knows the deal. PinkPop was unbelievable. I haven't watched the video, yet. Have you?"

"No. I'm too freaked out to watch that."

"Doc just received the pro-shot version. Do you want to grab Sonya and Maria and watch it in our suite? Just the band."

"Yes!"

"Doc, we're out. The band wants to have a band-only viewing party of the PinkPop show. Do I have that?"

"I'll send it to ya right now. Great work today."

"Backatcha, Doc. You're the fucking best."

The pajama party in the Princess Suite at the hotel started with Bloody Marys, Mimosas, and room service breakfast. Once everybody was comfortable and adequately prepared, Deadëye dimmed the lights and pressed the button. The band took a ride.

Nobody said a word or moved for 75 minutes. After Charlotte launched her Les Paul into the crowd and the closing credits ran, the band sat in stunned shock until Sonya said, "We're the greatest band on the fucking planet."

Maria found a bottle of tequila and poured shots for everyone. Charlotte was trembling and holding on to Deadëye for dear life. The words Deadëye whispered into Charlotte's ears, nobody will ever know.

"That was the best fucking rock 'n' roll show I've ever seen in my life," Sonya announced. "Maria held down the bottom end like a motherfucking champion, Deadëye murdered all 40 or 50 thousand motherfuckers in the audience with his commanding, frontman presence. I kept shit from getting out of control in the back. And Charlotte told the whole planet—meet the new boss."

"I'm so fucking proud of all of us," Maria said.

Deadëye was in tears. "Goddamn, that was good. Fuck!"

Charlotte said, "Let's watch that again."

The band was more animated and talkative on the second pass. For the third viewing, the band invited everybody they knew in Stockholm, including the press people they'd been avoiding.

After the fourth showing, Doc booted everyone out of the suite except the band and bid the emotionally spent foursome adieu. The band collapsed on the suite's bed in a heap of mutual admiration.

Deadëye awoke to find three naked women in the party shower covered in soapy hands.

"I need coffee," Deadëye grumbled.

"Drink some orange juice and take your vitamins," his wife said. Deadëye double-bolted the door and joined the band in their morning cleansing ritual. *Thursday in Stockholm*, Deadëye thought to himself.

The fearless foursome pushed the button and took the elevator ride to the ground-floor breakfast buffet. Six bottles of Prosecco later, Doc arrived with good news.

"None of the bands on the bill Saturday wanna follow you guys on stage, so you're headlining again."

"That's something Deadëye will never do, fear any other band," Sonya said. "Those bands are pussies."

Maria added, "Saturday nights belong to Deadëye, wherever the fuck we go."

Charlotte couldn't help but say, "Pearl is the color—"

"No!" screamed Maria and Sonya.

Deadëye announced a toast. "We are the best band. We have more fun than anyone. I love you all. We are Deadëye!"

Doc reported, "This shit's starting to get really fun. The Gibson people are on the same plane as Eyeball and Pearl!"

"Did we know the Gibson people were coming?"

"No, but I told Eyeball to bring 'em to dinner."

"Perfect."

"This just in," Doc announced. "The Australian writer at the party last night wrote, *I wanted to hate that band and those people so much, but their live show is un-fucking-believable.*"

"We're the best band on the fucking planet," Sonya announced. "I treasure every minute we are together. You bastards."

"Pearl is the—"

"No!"

Doc disappeared and sent Deadëye a text—*Meet me in the lobby right now*

Deadëye excused himself and went searching for a loo.

"We're headlining again in Berlin. That's two weeks from Saturday. They're offering us the Sunday headlining spot in Nuremberg, as well—some emo band canceled. And, if we want to cement your place in history, we can do an in-store appearance at a record store on Friday in Berlin. The odds are, we'll cause a riot."

"Let's do it at midnight."

"Talk to Charlotte, first. She's the one under the microscope here."

"When do you need an answer?"

"After Sofia says she'll film it all."

"You're a sick man, Doc."

"We're showing the PinkPop video after dinner—I booked the hotel cinema. You won't believe how great the footage is on that big screen. The Gibson guys are confirmed."

"Do we know anybody in Berlin willing to jump on an airplane this afternoon and join us for dinner and a movie?"

"Yes."

"Invite the record store guys, too."

"Consider it done."

Deadëye returned to the breakfast table and announced

another toast. "Ladies and gentlemen, you'll never forget this day, we're gonna have so much fun. At 2 p.m. we're walking across the street to our first stop, the world-famous Abba Museum! Round two: the Avicii Experience! Round three: happy hour! Round four: dinner with a few of our dear old friends and a few of our amazing new friends! Round five: a very special film screening in the hotel cinema!"

"Woo-hoo!" somebody said.

"We are Deadëye. We play rock 'n' roll!"

The band's emotions were on a hair-trigger, no matter how many flasks they downed in the Abba Museum. When Deadëye and Charlotte found out there was such a thing as the Abba Choir they demanded Doc arrange for the Abba Choir to perform as backup vocalists during the encore at the Saturday show.

"We're not making it to the Avicii thing today, are we?" Deadëye asked Doc.

"No, there's no way we can get the ladies out of the gift shop anytime soon," Doc surmised. "Let's go downstairs and grab a drink. Sofia and her crew will be here in a few and we want to intercept her on the way in."

Sure enough, amid their first round of martinis on the patio outside the Abba Museum, Sofia, her husband, and a couple of their statuesque Swedish friends arrived. Deadëye and Doc greeted the group, laid out the evening's itinerary, and handed out tickets to the museum. Deadëye told Sofia how excited Charlotte was to be seeing her again. All systems go.

"Should we join them inside?" Deadëye asked Doc.

"No," Doc responded as martini round two arrived, "Sofia's husband looked thirsty. They'll be joining us out here in 20 minutes."

Deadëye visited the water closet to inhale some powders with motivational powers. Back on the patio Doc scribbled notes on a napkin. "What's that?" Deadëye asked.

"My introduction for the film tonight," Doc responded. "This shit will make us $10 million. Watch."

"I'll watch!" Deadëye promised.

"You need to work on the after-dinner toast at the restaurant," Doc said. "That'll double it."

"What do I say?" Deadëye asked.

"I'll text it to you."

Sofia's husband and the Swedish dude joined Doc and Deadëye on the patio. "They'll be in there for hours," husband Tom said.

"What's going on?" Deadëye asked.

"Abba's costume designer and the museum's curator are in there," Tom said. "They're joining us for dinner and the movie."

"Holy fuck!" Deadëye said.

Swedish guy, Karl, said, "Welcome to Sweden, gentlemen. Skål!"

Sonya joined the group on the patio. "We cleaned out the gift shop and the museum sold us a bunch of cool shit they had in the back room," Sonya reported. "Wait until you see your outfit for the encore Saturday, Deadëye."

"Are we having fun, yet?" Deadëye asked Sonya.

Yes," she replied. "I need cocaine." All four of the bros at the table reached for their pockets.

"The Japanese, Australians, and group from Berlin are meeting us here any minute," Doc reported.

"Where's Cam?" Deadëye asked Doc.

"Cam's been busy with Charlotte's circus friend. Right now he's having the tour bus detailed, then he's picking us up here and driving us all to dinner."

"Perfect," Deadëye said. "Where's dinner?"

"Frantzén, I've booked the entire place."

Tom said, "That's the best restaurant in the world."

"That's fucking right," Doc said. "The best band in the fucking world deserves the best fucking restaurant in the world. Wait until you see the movie tonight."

Doc knows how to make motherfuckers pay attention, Deadëye said to himself as he read the minds of their drinking buddies who were wondering, *Who the fuck are these people?*

Travelers arrived from the airport, local Swedish press joined the fiesta, and the Deadëye ladies emerged from the museum clothed in spectacular Abba-style garb, preceded by Sofia and Karl's partner, Ava, who was operating a Super-8 camera. Just as the Abba Museum duo finished locking the doors and joined the party, Cam arrived in the Deadëye Express. Doc lied and told everybody the bus was not theirs. Once Cam and crew finished filling 30 glasses of champagne for the assembled group, Cam emerged from the bus wearing a train conductor's outfit and announced, "All aboard!"

Doc revealed the evening's itinerary on the way to the restaurant, Deadëye kept the guests' glasses filled with champagne, the record store dudes from Berlin stared at the scene with googly eyes, and the Deadëye ladies put on a fashion show.

Tom asked Deadëye and Doc, "Did you plan this?"

Doc replied, "Not really. We kinda just let shit happen."

"Plans are no fun," Deadëye added.

Doc told Deadëye, "When we stop, I'm jumping out and making sure everything's all set inside. Make a toast, thank everyone for being here, when I give Cam the sign he'll open the door and announce our arrival."

While Deadëye delivered a heartfelt toast to the assembled maniacs on the bus, Doc greeted every member of the restaurant's staff with an envelope of 5,000 krona and admired tables set with bottles of wine, liquor, and the appropriate accessories. Doc sent Cam the signal, the Deadëye Express passengers disembarked and entered the restaurant guided inside by a line of a half-dozen servers genuinely thrilled to meet their new friends.

The band members and Doc circulated, greeting and meeting old and new friends. Doc invited the Japanese and Australian press maniacs to tag along for the entire European tour. Deadëye arranged for a second, late-night showing of the PinkPop film that evening for the restaurant's staff. Lifelong friends were made over what was, indeed, the greatest meal anyone in that room had ever experienced. Since Cam was hammered, a relief driver appeared after dessert to ferry the sated diners to the band's hotel where the cinema's bartenders wisely offered self-serve bottles of vodka frozen into blocks of ice.

"It's a good thing we have cocaine," Sonya said. "This party is nuts."

MOVIE TIME! Doc set the scene, the film lit up the screen, high-volume rock 'n' roll rattled the chandeliers, and nobody in that room blinked for 75 minutes. The Deadëye ladies experienced what some might call post-traumatic stress PinkPop syndrome. Charlotte curled up in a fetal position clawing at Deadëye. The Abba Museum people stared at the screen in stunned silence for a couple of minutes after the end of the video. The jaded record store dudes and press people were stripped of their armor of know-it-all-ness. As a wise man once said, "The desired effect is what you get."

Sofia told Doc, "I'm calling you at 11 a.m." as she departed with her posse. The Abba Museum team said something similar on their way out. Doc announced the 2 a.m. second showing of the film and circulated amongst the crowd showing the world what an excellent host looks like as dessert carts and fire-breathing burlesque dancers provided intermission nutrition and entertainment. The band retreated to the Princess suite to decompress.

"Was I the only one in the theater not getting fingered?" Deadëye asked, in an attempt to break the tension amongst the band. He shouldn't have asked.

"No," Maria said. "I was getting fisted."

Fortified, energized, and without the Abba costumes, Deadëye, the band, exploded out of the elevator into the hotel lobby at 2 a.m. ready to rock. With the band's new besties in the Frantzén crew, some off-duty hotel staff, and assorted members of the Stockholm intelligentsia added to the menagerie in the house, Doc did his best P.T. Barnum-on-acid intro and the shit went down again. Like a motherfucker.

The late show was a lot looser than the midnight show. A good time was had by all. Doc asked Deadëye, "What do you think about showing the video in Berlin?"

"What do you think?"

"Fuck no," Doc said. "We bought the rights to the footage and we're selling it to Sofia tomorrow for ten times what I paid for it."

"I am in the presence of a God among men," Deadëye told Doc.

"Yes, you fucking are. Don't you forget it. We have nothing on the schedule after the Saturday show until the record store thing two weeks from tomorrow in Berlin," Doc said.

"We need time off to do regular shit before the three-days-in-a-row Germany deal," Deadëye said.

"Deadëye, you're working a total of six or seven hours the entire weekend, to be completely realistic," Doc said. "Be a big boy and help build Charlotte's confidence."

"Doc, that's a great idea."

"The Abba people just sent me a text," Doc said. "We'll see them tomorrow for breakfast. They say they're bringing surprises."

"What the fuck does that mean?" Deadëye wondered aloud.

Well, what it meant was that the Abba people brought a couple of the Abba people who demanded to see the film again while furiously taking notes.

"What the fuck are these people doing?" Deadëye asked Doc.

"Who knows? They're on our team, in the posse, working for us at this point. Just like all those fuckers in the press we hung out with yesterday. Deadëye is in the process of conquering Stockholm and we're really not working that hard. We haven't even played our first festival gig here. Relax, enjoy the show, that buzzing in your head is the sound of thousands of cash registers ringing."

"Every band on the planet will be trying to steal you from me," Deadëye said.

"You and me are fifty-fifty partners in Eyedöc Management, LLC. "

"I didn't know that."

"If you want me to do it and I wanna do it, I'll do it. I can't see that happening anytime soon. By the way, we get all the parking money in Germany."

"Holy shit."

"That money goes to Eyedöc Management, LLC."

"Do you ever sleep, Doc?"

"Like a motherfucking baby. This shit is like a new Disneyland every fucking day."

The Abba team stood up and marched over to Deadëye and Doc as soon as the PinkPop video ended. "It's time for your fitting, Mr. Deadëye."

Deadëye looked confused. With a smile on his face, Doc said, "Relax, enjoy the show."

The Abba people clothed Deadëye in his Stockholm encore outfit, he said, "I'll be right back." In the Princess Suite, Deadëye awakened his bride, who screamed in sheer hilarity and ecstasy when she saw her man dressed like an Abba member circa 2030. *Like a new Disneyland every fucking day*, Deadëye's brain told him.

Doc invited Deadëye and Charlotte downstairs for a private lunch on the terrace. The trio turned off all electronic devices and enjoyed each others' company with very little business discussed. After lunch, Doc said, "Let's go for a walk."

Doc led Charlotte and Deadëye out the back door of the hotel and into the building across the way. Through a set of heavy curtains appeared a magnificent theater.

"Oh my God," Charlotte said as she spun slowly in circles admiring the room.

"What the fuck is this?" Deadëye asked Doc.

"Cirkus. Capacity 1,700. Let's go."

Doc led Charlotte and Deadëye back outside through a real-life-ish Swedish village to an outdoor amphitheater with a giant wooden windmill next to the stage. "This is Sollidenscenen."

"Cool. Thanks, Doc," Deadëye said.

"Sofia wants to produce a documentary of this tour. She wants to film a show in Cirkus next Friday then a free show in the amphitheater Sunday."

Deadëye looked at his wife and asked, "What do you think—"

"Fuck yeah!" Charlotte screamed.

The Abba people and Charlotte's circus friends got busy planning the indoor show at Cirkus. *Yay, let's play dress-up!* Deadëye thought to himself.

The free show in the outdoor amphitheater would be devoid of theatrics—pure, unadulterated rock 'n' roll. Loud as fuck. Guaranteed to piss off the neighbors. With an airship known as Goodyear Europa floating overhead.

Charlotte left to hang with Sonya and Maria at their happy place, the Abba Museum. Deadëye asked Doc, "Did Sofia buy the PinkPop footage?"

"I don't think you know who you're talking to," Doc said with a giant smile on his face.

"Let's give everybody a bonus," Deadëye told Doc.

"Great idea. The Abba people are showing your wife a new line of merch they stayed up all night designing."

"What do you think about that?" Deadëye asked Doc.

"I think it might be a good idea. We'll see what happens. Don't get your hopes up."

For the first time, Deadëye didn't believe Doc was being completely honest with him. Deadëye looked Doc squarely in his dead eyes and asked him, "Motherfucker, what do you really think about the Abba fucks designing a line of Deadëye merch?"

"We're gonna make millions."

"Is there anything worth more than Abba cred?"

"No."

"Are The Doors a good band?"

"Fuck no."

"Okay, relax, Doc. Right answer. Just testing."

Doc said, "The only fucking thing that could make The Doors any worse would be to add that little fuck Glenn Danzig on vocals."

"Let's make that happen."

Well, some people blame Doc for sending The Doors on the road with Glenn Danzig as their vocalist. And some people praise Doc for booking the private plane that crashed into the side of a mountain in the Canadian Rockies after The

Doors show at the place where the Blue Jays lost the World Series to the Colorado Rockies. And some people wonder why there are so many Rockies. As a wise woman named Madonna once said, "Life is a mystery." Word.

Back on Earth, Charlotte interrupted the dream nine billion people have ending with both Glenn Danzig and The Doors meeting their demise like a retired basketball player did on a foggy day in a helicopter on his way to Calabasas.
"What's the festival called we're playing Saturday?" Charlotte asked.
"LOLLAPALOOZA," Doc answered.
In unison, Deadëye and Charlotte asked/screamed, "We're headlining LOLLAPALOOZA?"
"Yeah," Doc answered. "It's not PinkPop, but it'll do."

At LOLLAPALOOZA Stockholm, half the audience got it and half the audience didn't. Because it was one of those weird European festival set-ups where there were two stages side-by-side and attendees were committed to one side or the other upon entry. Deadëye murdered the poor cunts camping in that muddy field in front of their stage, then resurrected them with the encore, *Dancing Eye*, which saw the band in its silly Abba outfits, with the Abba Choir's backing, light the comatose campers on fire. Like champions.
Back in the hotel, the band assessed their injuries—physical and emotional—and self-medicated accordingly.
"That shit was fucking weird," Sonya said. "I think we need to get weirder."

Deadëye and Doc agreed and only trusted one other person's subjective opinion of Deadëye. So they sent Sonya to hang with the Abba people, the Canadian circus people, and Sofia for three days to hammer out the details for the Cirkus show.

"We gotta do something different at Cirkus," Doc told Charlotte and Maria. "Let go, let God."

"But, Sonya's a drummer," Maria said.

"So?" Doc asked.

"She's Asian," Maria added.

Charlotte started to say something and Doc cut her off. "All I know about Sonya is this. I watched Sonya murder a machine gun-wielding special forces fuck with her bare hands. She gouged his eyeballs out with her titanium fingernails, eviscerated the bastard with a fish hook, and dumped the dying cunt in the Gulf of fucking Mexico. Then she poured a five-gallon bucket of pigs' blood into the water to attract every shark in the gulf. Laughing her ass off the whole time. My professional advice is, let's let Sonya handle this one."

"Isn't Stockholm our most important market?" dumbfuck Deadëye asked.

"Uh, no," Doc answered. "Less than a million people live here. For perspective, Tokyo has 14 million people. Stockholm rules, however, this town is a tiny stepping stone in the whole scheme of things."

"We have a scheme?" Deadëye asked.

"Well, we have a—"

"We have a scheme!" Maria screamed as she and Charlotte hugged it out.

Because he's an evil bastard, Doc brought out some even more powerful vocabulary for the ladies.

"After the scheme, we're planning a heist."

S ONYA'S APPROACH TO ALL THINGS was rooted in brutal honesty, transparency, and inclusiveness. Meaning she involved her homies in every step of the decision-making process. Charlotte and Maria joined Sonya to devise the heist scheme for the Cirkus show.

"The Abba people want us to dress in black and white," Sonya said.

"Amazing!" Charlotte exclaimed. "That would be totally awesome if this were 1996 and we were The Hives?"

"Do you have a better idea?" Sonya asked Charlotte.

"Hold on," Charlotte told Sonya as she appeared to search for a Legendary Pokemon on her phone. "Breaking news! Doc just fired the Abba fucks."

Sonya screamed, "*YOU* fired the Abba fucks!"

"Sonya, think about it," Charlotte said. "We're talking about Abba here. If me and Doc ever fire the Black Sabbath people, or, since we're in Sweden, any of the Viagra Boys, feed us to the sharks. Personally. I believe *Bjorn Again* is the best Black Sabbath album. And I told Geezer that. He blocked my number after that. Anyway, in the whole scheme of things, Abba is corny satin jacket-type shit. I don't deserve to die for firing the cunts responsible for giving the world the Swedish Bee Gees."

"Who the fuck do we know who can make shit happen by Saturday?" Maria asked.

"Let's talk in the morning," Charlotte said. "Mime is money."

Charlotte's Canadian circus posse lived on a higher spiritual plane than the music business losers were accustomed to. Nobody in Sweden ever needed Abba. Nobody in Sweden expected the awesomeness Montreal's best acrobats delivered to Cirkus. The band's massive audio system may or may not have been responsible for the chunks of ceiling masked by clouds of confetti falling from the arena's sky. Shit happens when people don't pack the right voltage adapters when traveling.

The free outdoor amphitheater show on Sunday afternoon stood in marked contrast to the festival show and the Cirkus extravaganza. The band tore through their entire set barely taking a breather between songs. Mainly because Doc and Deadëye chose to rent the largest sound system ever seen in Scandinavia as a gift to the people of Stockholm and beyond. Ninety minutes after it all began, Deadëye, Charlotte, and Doc were in a helicopter over the Baltic Sea.

27 SHAKE IT UP

"LET'S CLOSE THE L.A. OFFICE," Doc said, one day, at breakfast.

"Why?"

"Eyeball and Pearl are useless. And, without an office in America, there are certain tax advantages."

"Let me think about it," Deadëye said. Three seconds later he asked, "Why didn't we do this sooner?"

The wise man he is, Doc and his reverse headhunters already had positions at other music industry firms lined up for Eyeball and Pearl. An attorney with paperwork to sign and envelopes full of cash along with baseball bat-toting dudes and a locksmith stood in the doorway of the Deadëye offices as Doc delivered the news.

"Adios, bitches!" Deadëye said as all business ties to America went *poof!*

"I never liked that place," Deadëye told Doc. "Can you get me citizenship in a civilized country?"

"Sure," Doc replied. "Sweden?"

"Ja."

"I don't know if you know this about me," Doc said, "but I'm always thinking."

"Wow," Deadëye said, "that's good to know. By your general appearance and demeanor, nobody would ever look at you and think to themselves, 'That dude is always thinking,' To be perfectly honest, you look like a child molester with Down's Syndrome. Not that there's anything wrong with that."

"Fuck you, Deadëye."

"Fuck you, Doc. Did your mom have any children that lived?"

"My brother plays bass in Stryper."

"So, the answer is no. I wish I had known how stupid you are before we went flying in your airplane."

"I passed my pilot's license examination on the fifth attempt, motherfucker. By the third time, everybody thought my name was Norm."

"That's not a compliment," Deadëye said. "You said you're always thinking. When you're thinking, what are you thinking about?"

"To be perfectly honest, most of the time I'm thinking about fried chicken."

"Like, a bucket from KFC or a sandwich from Popeye's?"

"Mostly, I think about the Colonel. When I was young, maybe 12 or 13, an older woman gave me a ride home from soccer practice. She had a bucket of Original Recipe in the back seat. Nothing weird happened, but the scent of those herbs and spices triggered some kind of hormones or whatever."

"So, your dick gets hard when you smell Original Recipe?"

"I'm not talking to you anymore, Deadëye."

"Personally, I've always found the Original Recipe to be more finger lickin' good than the Extra Crispy."

"Deadëye, when we go back on tour we're hiring the Lynyrd Skynyrd airplane people to fly us from town to town and the Steve Ray Vaughn helicopter people to do the short hops."

"Why don't we hire the 9/11 people and just get it over with?"

28 SPACE JAMS

THE GREAT THING ABOUT BEING CRAZY IS, you wear out your welcome pretty fast. Affording the opportunity to classify a hotel ejection as racism, thus escaping the payment.

"Sonya, do you watch South Park?" Doc asked on the tour bus rolling down the road to Deadëye's new Berlin hotel/German base of operations.

"Motherfucker, if you're about to call me Token, I'm about to murder your fat fucking ass."

"How? With Tai Chi?"

"Tai Chi. Krav Maga, CarJitsu."

"I prefer to murder drummers with TR-808, Oberheim DMX, LM-1—"

"I usually go with the AR-15 first," Sonya said.

"Have you seen that hot Korean drummer on YouTube?" Doc asked Sonya. "I can replace you with that Seoul sister like that."

"That's why you're a shitty manager, Doc," Sonya said. "A great manager, a Peter Grant, for example, would hire that half-cat/half-apple dude in Japan."

"Why?"

"Nobody sees the drummer. It doesn't fucking matter what the drummer looks like. Why pay extra for a hairless Korean nymphomaniacal supermodel?"

And, just like that, Deadëye's new gimmick for the post-Deutschland European festival dates would adopt the tried-and-true two-drummer lineup made popular by the worst bands of the 1970s. With a hairless Asian-fusion twist.

"Doc, we'll look like we're pandering to the Asian market with two female Asian drummers," Charlotte said. "Like we have yellow fever."

"It was Sonya's idea," Doc said. "We all agreed we should trust her judgment. Remember?"

"Don't get me wrong, Doc, I like Nina, she's very precise. Like a machine. But don't you think her nymphomania will be a problem on the road?" Charlotte asked.

To this day, Deadëye doesn't know if Charlotte ever received an answer to that question. Deadëye feigned food poisoning ran to the tour bus loo, and buried his face in somebody's skanky used bath towel while Doc pretended to have a stroke. The funniest shit is the most dangerous shit, Jesus said, on that cross. If there is a God.

The band performed in front of a packed house at a small club in Berlin on Friday night then headed down the street to the record store for the midnight event. The band's Japanese ambassador/music journalist, Hiro, was a surprise visitor to Berlin.

"Why don't we hire Hiro to run the Japanese operation?" Deadëye asked Doc.

"We don't need to," Doc said. "He's already working for us and we don't even have to pay him."

"Let's hire him and turn him into the most powerful man in the Japanese music industry," Deadëye suggested. "We lease a storefront in Shinjuku, fill it with all the shit we have left over after the tour, and paint a portrait of Hiro as the motherfucking man in the worldwide music press. The man responsible for Deadëye's incredible success in Asia. Every indie band in the world will want to work with Fire Tornado Japan."

"Sounds good to me," Doc remarked. "I didn't know you wanted to be a retailer."

"The circus people know what to do with retail space," Deadëye said. "Let's get a bunch of photos with Hiro."

Sonya's new drum buddy, Nina, attended the concert in Berlin to observe the show and learn what the band was all about. There are so many different directions the rest of this part of the story could go right now. Let's just say, Nina was not a great driver and she failed to understand the subtleties of operating a motor vehicle in "foreign" countries. There is a wrong side of the road, for example, in every country.

Deadëye couldn't help himself as the band left the body identification event at the Berlin coroner's office. "Sonya, what do you think about adding a second bass player?" Much to his surprise, Sonya was not upset by Deadëye's crass, insensitive, back-handed remark about their deceased bandmate.

"Ya know," Sonya said, "Nina may have died young, but she lived a full life. A life full of cock. I've never seen anything like it. She was like Pearl on steroids. After the first few hours sharing a room with her, I was sore just watching her. The way she absolutely devoured every single penis in the neighborhood made me think she possessed some kind of cock-finding radar. I almost—"

"Thank you, Sonya," Charlotte said. "As soon as we find a Korean translator we'll add your comments to the card we're sending her family."

IN THEIR FREE TIME IN SWEDEN, Doc and Deadëye formulated a long-term plan for Deadëye and prepared a presentation for the band and Cam.

In the hotel conference room in Paris, Doc laid it all out. "We're doing this shit for 30 months. Every year we'll do thirty weeks of touring, ten weeks of rehearsals and recording, and twelve weeks of vacation. All of us are on salary, everybody gets a per-diem every day we're on the road or in the studio, and all the food/hotels are paid for on the road and in New Orleans. We split income from the band's live shows, record sales, publishing, and merch six ways—20% each for me, Charlotte, and Deadëye, and 13% each for Sonya, Maria, and Cam. Solo shit is separate."

"After Japan, we're on vacation until New Orleans in September. We work until Christmas, take six weeks off, meet again in New Orleans, hit the road for a while, take six weeks off, meet in New Orleans, repeat."

"We have five album cycles planned, right now we're in the middle of the first one. The second one starts after we're back from vacation in September."

"Any questions?"

"I have a comment," Sonya said. "I'm not going on a fucking vacation. We just barely started this shit."

Doc said, "The studio in New Orleans is all ours. If you want to do solo shit or start a country band and crank out a record, feel free."

"Let's make a record!" Maria told Sonya.

"I'm staying in Japan for a week to decompress," Doc explained, "cruising around Florida in my new boat for a couple of weeks, then setting up your next record."

Charlotte added, "We're going to see my parents in Montreal, then spending a month in Italy and Spain. In Spain we'll probably record some acoustic material and write songs for the band."

"What are you gonna do, Cam?" Deadëye asked.

"I'm going straight to Gibson Nashville and filling a few storage units with gear. Let me know if you need anything," Cam said. "And I'm becoming a country artist. Those fucking hillbillies will buy anything from a dude named Cam."

"That's a great idea, Cam," Doc said. "It sounds like we're launching a country music division, too."

29
GERMANY

Tasteless humor persisted throughout Germany, just like the tasteless food at the hotel breakfast buffet in Nuremberg.

"I miss Nina," Sonya said. "She always brought something fermented to breakfast."

Charlotte spit out her sausage. Sonya appeared offended. She stared at Charlotte and said, "I was talking about kimchee, you pervert."

And that's the way most of the rest of the European tour went. Shows in Paris, Barcelona, and Madrid were loud, heavy, and legendary. The two triumphant shows in London put an exclamation point on an incredible eight weeks of festivities.

"Only one person died?" Sonya said as the band sailed over the Alps on the way to Perth.

"We tried," Charlotte said.

"There are a lot of cunts in Paris I wish I'd killed," Maria said.

Deadëye asked Doc, "Should we talk about this shit on an airplane these days?"

"We are writers," Doc said. "We make movies, we write songs. Sometimes with titles such as, *Blow This Motherfucker Out of the Sky* and—"

"I get it. We can always tour Europe on a riverboat when we're on the no-fly list," Deadëye said.

"You're right," Doc said. "I have offers to do some cruise ships and casinos."

"My initial thought is, we do all of the casinos, state and county fairs, and cruise ships all over middle America in five years," Deadëye said. "One year, that's all we do."

"That's a great idea."

"You know Sofia's going to make Charlotte an offer she can't refuse to do a film, right?" Deadëye asked Doc. "It's inevitable and it'll probably happen in about six months."

"I know. I've heard some shit. She's finalizing the screenplay, working on her co-star," Doc said. "She's gone by this time next year, Deadëye. No matter what you do, you're gonna lose her."

Deadëye stirred the ice cubes in his gin and tonic, knew full well his psychic advisor was right, and said, "Fuck you, Doc."

"There's not a goddamned thing you or anybody else can do. Push that button, take that ride, don't do anything stupid. She'll be back someday after she's been through the Hollywood wringer for a couple of years."

"Fuck you."

"Maintain your artistic credibility and don't let any of the bullshit get in the way of the music and you'll be fine. People come and go."

"How'd we do in the parking business in Europe?" Deadëye asked Doc.

"We couldn't take all the cash with us, so we bought some parking lots."

"Wow!"

"Do you know how much money the dumbfucks running those electric car companies will pay to install their bootleg electrical outlets in a parking lot?"

"A shitload?"

"No! A truckload," Doc said. "And, they cover the whole place with solar panels, so we're selling electricity, too."

"Damn…"

"Don't get me started on these electric flying taxis. You will shit when you see the numbers those venture capital cunts are talking about."

"What's the end game with this whole band thing, here?"

"I'll be living in a house with a boat dock in Connecticut, you'll be living in a castle surrounded by a moat in France, award-winning actress Charlotte will be getting married and divorced over and over again in Beverly Hills, Sonya will be starring in a fucked-up transgender version of an acrobatic traveling punk rock circus, Maria will be killed in some kind of equestrian accident, and Cam will be an outlaw biker country music star."

"What about—"

"Hiro will send us quarterly checks from Japan. We'll own stock in every electric car company, every flying car company, and every drone package delivery company. Plus we'll retain a majority interest in the parking lot company."

"That sounds great."

"It won't happen by itself. The next couple of years are critical. We build on every success. We learn and grow. We maintain momentum—"

"Have you been reading *Good to Great*?"

"As a matter of fact…"

THREE
HEAD EAST

30
AUSTRALIA & JAPAN

DEADËYE TRANSITIONED from giant festival stages to theater stages in Australia and Japan save for the final weekend at Fuji Rock Festival. The acoustic show returned as the opening act. Four nights in Australia, four nights in Japan, then the long festival weekend in the mountains of Western Japan. Thanks to the Australian and Japanese press people Deadëye feted across Europe, all of the headlining shows sold out and the Japanese fans welcomed the band's first big Japanese festival show enthusiastically.

"You were great last night," Charlotte told Deadëye after the final show of the tour.

"As were you, my love," Deadëye responded. "Can we send the film crew home, now? And the little person?"

The band scattered in all different directions. Deadëye and Charlotte spent a couple of days in Tokyo doing non-music business stuff. Museums, shopping, drinking, drinking...

"I wish I never had to see another airport again," Charlotte told Deadëye the day before the exceptionally talented and beautiful couple were scheduled to leave Japan behind.

"Without airports, we would have never met," Deadëye told Charlotte.

"I didn't meet Charles because of an airport," Charlotte said. "I met Charles because I fell in love with a fake character named Deadëye."

"Is there a difference?" Deadëye asked his wife. "Am I not the same person?"

Charlotte considered her remarks carefully, and said, "I feel like I am always cheating on one of you. I feel so guilty all of the time."

"Do you feel like you need to be punished?" Deadëye asked.

"Will you?" Charlotte begged. "Please? Now?"

All it took to convince Charlotte she was a very bad girl was an afternoon purchasing and experimenting with leather and rubber products followed by a couple of hours in a Tokyo dungeon. Then an evening doing that very same thing. And a late night, third round of the same, only different. Deadëye wondered to himself if he and Charlotte were breaking new ground, pioneering, in other words, while engaged in behaviors the most creative minds were unlikely to have ever imagined in the first-class restroom of a 787. Technically, certain of their activities can and are considered medical procedures, so it's possible they were not the first, in some cases. The combination, sequencing of events, and execution are what made Charlotte and Deadëye/Charles stand apart from all the rest.

"WE DID IT," CHARLES SAID TO HIS BEAUTIFUL WIFE. "We did it, Mrs. King. We started in New Orleans, conquered Europe, destroyed Australia, and nuked Japan."

"And we are closer to each other than ever before," Charlotte said. "Don't believe Doc—I will never leave you. Nothing can tear us apart."

"You will always challenge me, Charlotte. Even if you don't, you will, in my fucked up brain connected to a heart expecting to be broken."

"That's your fucking problem."

"You're right."

"What's the worst thing that can happen?"

"I don't know."

"That's what she said."

"Who let the dogs out?"

"We're buying a castle in France. With a moat. The dogs can't get out."

"Bark like a dog."

"Arf!"

"Where did I put your collar?"

"In your checked luggage. With my leash."

"Why must I feel like that? Why must I chase the cat?"
"It's nothing but the dog in you."
"Do fries come with that shake?"
"Hit me with your best shot."
"You dropped a bomb on me."
"I will always love you."
"Love me two times."
"Stop, in the name of love."
"Love will keep us together."
"Why do stars fall down from the sky?"
"Every time I walk by?"
"I guess I'm lyin' to myself."
"It's just you and no one else."
"The song remains the same."
"You give love a bad name."
"I'm a smooth criminal."
"Welcome to the jungle."
"Your kiss is on my lips."
"Hips don't lie."
"I get knocked down, and I get back up again."
"I only have eyes for you."
"Sometimes when we touch…"
"The honesty's too much?"
"No stop signs, no speed limit."
"Nothing's gonna slow us down."
"First we take Manhattan."
"Then we take Berlin."
"You know you're a cute little heartbreaker."
"And you know you're a sweet little lovemaker"
"I'm not the only soul who's accused of hit and run."

"Tire tracks all across your back, I can see you've had your fun."

"If you ever hurt me, everybody you know will want to kill you."

"If you ever hurt me, everybody will blame me, anyway. How the fuck did all this happen, anyway?"

"I manifested it," Charlotte said. "It's really not that difficult. I knew you would make me happy. I knew I could make you happy. So I made it happen."

"So, you prayed on top of a mountain, or something like that?"

"No, silly. I went to Philadelphia and told Gritty what I wanted."

"Gritty?" Deadeye exclaimed. "The hockey team mascot, Gritty?"

Charlotte stared at Deadëye for a long, tense moment. "When I see it, I know it, Charles. I knew Gritty would make it happen."

"You are the most remarkable woman who has ever lived, Charlotte. If I can't have you, I don't want nobody, baby."

31 CANADIA

"I CAN'T WAIT TO SEE YOUR FAMILY," Deadëye said as the 787 Dreamliner descended into the Montreal airport.

"It's okay if you have sex with my sisters," Charlotte said.

"What? I was talking about your parents."

"I'll ask, but that's kinda weird."

And that's the way the Canadian leg of the holiday started. Charlotte's sisters were waiting for Deadeye in little schoolgirl uniforms a couple of sizes too small eager to receive their punishment.

"I like being dominated by American men," one sister said as she handed Deadëye a roll of duct tape.

When people told him the entertainment business was for suckers, there was no future in music, stay in school, Deadëye always said, "Suck my dick!" Charles didn't know why he remembered that tidbit of information from his past as Charlotte's sisters took turns competing to make Little Charlie disappear into their faces as even the most durable eyeliner and lipstick from the line of cosmetics promoted by Armenian reality television show stars failed at its only job —memories are weird that way. And what the hell else was Deadëye gonna do for three hours while Charlotte's stylist pumped her aura full of carcinogenic hair products? Watch hockey on television?

Ten days was all it took for Deadëye to miss the band, the business, the road, and all of the awesomeness he'd worked a lifetime to turn his dreams into reality.

"Who died?" Doc asked as he answered Deadëye's phone call.

"Nina."

"That was months ago."

"Where are you?"

"Tokyo. We found a killer location for the store. The circus freaks and Hiro are turning it into the retail personification of Deadëye. You're never gonna believe this shit."

"Fuck!" Deadëye exclaimed. "I'm not ready for a vacation right now. I wanna keep kicking ass and building our band!"

"Good," Doc said. "We're doing a grand opening celebration for ten days in the middle of your New Orleans sessions. If you wanna do it, and I would if I were you, bring the band over here and play live at the opening fiesta. Then spend a couple of weeks playing smaller markets here you've never been to."

"Fuck it, let's skip New Orleans and spend a month in Japan instead of Louisiana!"

"Run it by Mrs. King. I know everybody else will be all about it. Cam's already here, I'll get him started turning the basement into a studio."

"Okay, I'll call you after the hockey game."

"Hockey game?"

"Yeah, you don't wanna know…"

Deadëye gave Charlotte the 411 on Tokyo, Charlotte said, "Fuck yeah! Let's go to Tokyo right now!"

"How about we spend a few days in Hawaii on our way to Japan? We'll just be in the way right now. Doc needs some time to set up shows for us."

"Fuck that, Charles. I'm too excited to do vacation shit now."

Everybody was on board for the quick return to Japan except Sonya—she decided to become a monk for a few weeks back in her homeland of Minnesota."

"Who can play drums, Doc?"

"It's covered. The half-cat/half-apple guy is already here."

"Dude, that motherfucker is the best! Don't tell Charlotte, I want it to be a surprise. We're on our way, Charlotte is too excited about everything to relax."

"Your wife will lose her mind when she sees the Deadëye Megastore Tokyo. Between you and me, Hiro has seven more locations lined up all over Japan. His father is a billionaire real estate mogul. He owns skyscrapers all over Asia."

"Did we know that before we made him our band's best friend?"

"Not a clue. We just knew he was crazy enough to hang out with us," Doc said. "By the way, if you wanna sell the parking lots we have a willing and able buyer."

"Any more terrible news?" Deadëye asked Doc, sarcastically.

"I'll let you know when you get here. You can't handle the truth."

"Sell that shit. Show me the money!"

"I'll sell the parking lots if you surprise your wife with a castle for your anniversary."

"When's that?"

With parking lot money in a "bank" somewhere in the Bahamas, Deadëye tasked Charlotte's sisters with the secret European mission to find a castle.

"Oh. My. God, Charles! Colette and Musette will be so excited!"

"Musette?" Deadëye asked. "Who's Musette?"

"Colette's identical twin!"

"Oh, that explains everything. I thought Colette was almost as insatiable as my wife. Why didn't anybody tell me there were two of them?"

"Charles, you know nothing about your wife and our family—your family."

"We are family?"

"I got all my sisters with me, Charles. I got all my sisters with me."

Deadëye did the inadvisable by calling Cam to see how he was holding up in Tokyo.

"Dude, these guys Hiro knows over here are the most amazing motherfuckers I've ever met," Cam said. "I tell them to build a stage. I go grab a cup of coffee, when I come back it's already done. Perfectly."

"Do we own the whole building?" Deadëye asked.

"Hiro does."

"Tell them to build a strip club on the roof."

"I already did. It's amazing."

"How's the studio?"

"We bought all of the vintage gear on the planet. And it's studios, plural. Three studios in the basement. We're turning the sub-basement into a cinema and orchestral scoring room."

"Anything else?"

"Just your basic, everyday stuff. The half-cat/half-apple guy set up his drums yesterday and ran through 40 of your songs. And they're testing flying electric cars on the roof. This place is at least 300 years ahead of New Orleans. I'm moving here."

"What about the country thing?"

"I asked myself, 'Cam, do you want to be surrounded by cousin fuckers or live in the motherfucking future?' "

"The cousin-fucking past or the motherfucking future?"

"That was the determining factor. If I want to see a bunch of inbreeding going on I can spend a week in Florida. West Palm Beach is the inbreeding capital of the world, according to four out of five doctors surveyed."

"Do you have a plan to surprise Charlotte when she meets the half-cat/half-apple drummer?"

"I thought I did. AppleCat met Gritty yesterday and they both disappeared. Do we have medical insurance? I'm seriously haunted by the images in my brain of what those two might be doing to each other."

"Are you using drugs, Cam?"

"Every day. #alldaylong."

"That's not the problem, then. Have you been to one of those soapland places?"

"No. The hotel has free soap."

"Hand your phone to Hiro."

"Deadëye-san, so wonderful to speak with you."

"Stop that, Hiro, I'm a married man. Do you need anything?"

"Colombian hookers and Goldfish."

"Goldfish? Like, Pepperidge Farm Goldfish?"

"Yes! Yes! We do not have such things in Japan."

"Why don't we cut a deal with Pepperidge Farms to be the exclusive distributor of Goldfish in Japan?"

"You fucking Americans."

"What's wrong?"

"You fucking Americans and your ideas. Japanese people are not allowed to have ideas. We are programmed to live our lives as robots."

"The nail that sticks up gets hammered down."

"Exactly. Do you want me to tell you which Colombian hookers I want or do you think you can figure it out for yourself?"

"First of all, tell me which flavor of Goldfish you want. Those Pepperidge people pump out a new flavor every day. And send me a link to the Cartagenans. And, more importantly, take Cam to the soapland. That dude gets weird after a few months without Asian pussy."

"We're building a soapland and an image club on the eleventh floor. Right across the hall from the bowling alley."

"Do you really need Colombians? In my experience, the Malaysians are less likely to do that scopolamine shit."

"Ya know, I think you're right, Deadëye. As soon as you get here we need to go check out the location I've found for Deadëye Megastore Malaysia."

"Twist my arm, Hiro. Twist my arm."

"What the fuck is this?" Charlotte screamed as she shoved a newspaper in Deadëye's face and demanded an explanation.

"I was hungry."

"Hungry Singer Arrested?" Charlotte yelled. "How the fuck did you get arrested at a Burger King?"

"They wouldn't let me have it my way."

"What?"

"Burger King told us all as kids growing up we could have it our way," Deadëye said. "There was no expiration date on the offer and no fine print limiting the scope of 'our way'."

"Don't even tell me—"

"Anal."

32
SOMEWHERE OVER A RAINBOW

Deadëye knew if it wasn't happening at that moment, it was just around the corner.

"What did you do to my sisters?" Charlotte asked. "They're acting so weird."

The blame came hard and heavy. "Do you want a list?" Deadëye asked Charlotte. "I can go from A to Z at least a few times."

"What the hell is the Z?" Charlotte asked.

"The Zebra," Deadëye answered.

"My sisters love you so much," Charlotte said. "They are so happy for me. They don't really care about my music or acting or anything like that."

"I brought you a friend," Deadëye said. "It's going to be a long flight. Close your eyes." Deadëye reached into his carry-on bag and pulled out a device guaranteed to comfort and amuse Charlotte during the 13-plus hours on the plane to Tokyo.

Charlotte opened her eyes and shrieked. "Gritty!" Mrs. King grabbed her new Gritty pillow, held it tight, laid down on the lie-flat airplane seat/bed, and fell asleep with a gigantic smile on her face. *Gritty does it again.*

The entire posse shocked Charlotte and Deadëye with their warm and boisterous meeting in the Tokyo Narita terminal. Charlotte demanded to see the Deadëye Megastore Shinjuku immediately. As soon as Charlotte walked through the doors she scanned the room silently and said, "Get me the fuck out of here." The crew walked across the street to the local izakaya and pounded sake as Charlotte stared out the window at the Deadëye flagship store. After a few drinks, Charlotte said, "It looks like a Japanese circus on acid in France."

"Are we ready to show Charlotte the studio?" Deadeye asked Doc.

"I'll get everything set up," Maria said as she ran across the street.

Deadëye had a new St. Vincent waiting for Charlotte in the control room of Deadëye Tokyo Studio One. Maria started playing bass, Deadëye cranked up his guitar, Charlotte struck her first chord on the new St. Vincent, and a drummer started a fill that seemed to last five minutes. "Who's playing drums?" Charlotte asked.

The drummer, cloaked in darkness in a corner of the room, kicked off *Voodoo Eyes* and the band joined in. After two verses, the band hit the chorus and Cam hit the lights in the studio revealing the half-cat/half-apple drummer. Charlotte's head exploded. *Life is but a dream.*

Doc asked Deadëye, "Have you checked your text messages?"

"No, what's up?" Deadëye asked.

Doc said, "Check your messages."

"What the fuck!" Deadëye screamed. Deadëye grabbed Doc and dragged him outside for a walk around the block.

Doc asked Deadëye, "What do you think?"

"What the fuck do you think I think?"

"You think I should wire the funds right fucking now," Doc said.

"Do we have time to fly to France before the grand opening bullshit here?" Deadëye asked.

"Go now. Right now."

"What do I tell her?"

"Doc says we need to go to France and meet a member of the royal family."

"Do they have one of those there?"

"Grab your wife, we need to be at the airport now. You'll wake up in Nice the day after tomorrow at 9 a.m."

"That's a badass castle. Can I afford it?"

"Motherfucker, that's not a castle. It's a fortress," Doc said. "We made $60 million each selling parking lots a couple of weeks ago. You need a fortress."

"I can't wait to hear the bullshit story you tell Charlotte when she asks why we have to get on a plane for 18 hours."

"You're in first class."

"You have a French investor who made all of his money in fine art who wants to give you $500 million for your songs and your retail empire."

"Jesus…"

"Her sisters are meeting you at the airport. They're convinced Charlotte will love the place, we're good."

"On the map, it looks like half the property is in France and half of it's in Italy."

"Perfect. As if buying a fucking fortress isn't complicated enough, already. The Italians fucking hate you, remember? You fucked up their whole party at the embassy in Stockholm."

"Just the government. The people of Italy don't hate people, they're too stupid for that."

"Don't worry, we'll form a shell company inside a shell company so nobody knows who you are."

"Who the fuck is our new drummer and why does he/she/it/they wear a silly costume?"

"It's not a costume."

"Please…"

"Is Gritty wearing a costume?"

"If you ever say one bad thing about Gritty I'll cut your dick off and make you eat it."

"You wouldn't be the first."

"Are we driving on the correct side of the road, Doc?"

"That's the least of your problems, Deadëye."

"Who is this man we are meeting called The Count?"

Doc and Deadeye laughed so hard they had problems breathing. Doc said, "He's a very successful art collector. He owns a lot of Hensons."

"And a few Rogers."

"I need drugs. You fucking weirdos are pissing me off."

Doc said, "I'm pretty sure he has some original Kangaroos."

"I've never heard of any of the artists you speak of," Charlotte said.

"That's why The Count is so wealthy," Doc said. "He only deals with artists who produce low numbers."

"When are we coming back?" Charlotte asked Deadëye.

"After we see The Count, you will tell me what you want to do and we can have our first fight."

"That's not very nice, Charles!"

"Charlotte, have I ever disappointed you?"

"No, you have not."

"I promise you, every single minute we spend in France will thrill you with delight."

"Will you give me diamonds bright?"

"For your love, I'd give the moon if it were mine to give"

"You fucking weirdos are killing my buzz," Doc said.

In unison, Deadëye and Charlotte said, "You hate us, 'cause you ain't us."

"Get out!" Doc screamed as we exited his car and ran to the Lufthansa gate.

"We're on a 747 to Frankfurt. First class."

"France doesn't have a single decent rock band."

"So, it's just like Canada, then."

"Very few places on our planet have good rock 'n' roll bands."

"Damn, I think you're right, Charlotte. America, England, Ireland, Sweden, Norway, Germany, Japan… I think that's it."

"Mexico."

"Australia."

"So, The Count would tell us, there are only, one, two…"

The silly sisters decided to hide in the back of the airport shuttle van behind a giant piece of cardboard for a few minutes, until the route to the fortress approached the Italian border, at which point the three jokers lowered the visual obstruction and started laughing. Charlotte turned around to see her sisters, glared at her husband, then screamed loud enough to scare the shit out of the driver.

"What the hell's going on around here?" Charlotte asked nobody in particular.

"We're going to see The Count!" Colette said.

Two hours later and after the thrill had completely gone, the airport shuttle bus driver pulled into a courtyard the size of a football stadium where a man and woman resembling real estate agents stood smiling those smarmy smiles real estate agents are trained to practice along with their scripts.

"Welcome Charlotte, would you like a drink?"

"Do you have any drugs?"

"But of course."

"That drive was hell," Charlotte told her sisters and Deadëye. "What the hell are we doing here?"

"Mrs. King, this is your fortress."

"My fortress?"

"I bought you a fortress."

"How do we ever get out of here?"

"Watch. Hey, real estate guy. We'll wire the funds right now if you'll include a Sikorsky."

"S-76B okay?"

"Yes."

"Let me make a phone call."

As the real estate weasel made a phone call, Charlotte's sisters grabbed her and ran into the fortress and weren't seen again for a while.

"What's that over there?" Deadeye asked the real estate lady as he pointed across the canyon.

"That's Italy," she said. "Tell Francois you want the helicopter, those two range rovers over there, and a $5 million price reduction."

"Who's Francois"

"The real estate guy."

"I don't like this place. Show us something closer to civilization."

"Get me the hell out of here, Charles!"

"Louise is taking us back to Nice in a helicopter."

"France sucks. Take me to Barcelona. We can send my stupid sisters back to Montreal."

"Okay. We can go back to Tokyo whenever. Or not. We'll be in Barcelona for happy hour. Here comes the helicopter!"

"I like Stockholm, but it's too cold and dark in the winter," Charlotte said. "I like Spain. I like Barcelona."

"We don't need to buy a home right now," Deadeye told Charlotte.

"Motherfucker, we need a home! We are homeless. We need one place we can call home. Not New Orleans, we go there to work. Not Montreal, these stupid bitches live there. I hate America, I hate France, I hate Italy, Australia has giant spiders and animals with pockets."

"Let's find a place in Barcelona. I know exactly where we want to be. We can spend as much time as you want there. We're supposed to be on vacation right now, anyway."

"Okay."

"We need a home, Charlotte, you're right."

"I have a big decision to make before we get to Barcelona, Charles."

"What's your dilemma?"

"Which one of these cunts do I kill first?" Charlotte said as she gestured toward her sisters.

"Kill me, Charlotte. I asked your sisters to find you a castle."

"Okay, I'll get that done tonight."

"I want to show you something on my phone."

"Not another dick pic."

Deadëye pulled up an image on his phone and showed it to Charlotte.

"Where did that come from?" Charlotte asked.

"We sold our parking lots."

"What parking lots?"

"The parking lots me and Doc bought in Europe."

"How do we keep making millions without doing any work?"

"Doc is a genius. You are a superstar. I convince smarter people than me to do crazy shit," Deadëye said. "We've earned more than $100 million in less than a year. Hiro's about to make us millions more. You're about to become a major movie star."

"We're never spending any of that money, Deadëye," Charlotte said. "We put that money in safe shit and we'll have $100,000 every month to spend. I don't give a fuck about castles, or shoes, or handbags, or any of the stupid shit. I know exactly what I want, I waited my whole life for it, the rest of this bullshit is meaningless, Charles."

"You need a puppy."

"I need a machete. Why are you always fucking with me? The apple/cat drummer, the surprise sisters, the castle—I'm not at all impressed."

"It's a good thing Gritty wasn't in Tokyo, then."

"He was probably busy buttfucking Captain Kangaroo."

"Ouch."

"Charles, I know everything about you. I know what you're thinking before you even think about thinking about it. This is my curse. A defect, not a feature. I would give anything to make it stop. Nobody likes a know-it-all. I've spent my life learning how to be stupid."

"Maybe you—"

"Shut the fuck up. Charles. I've told you a dozen times, you appeared, I wanted you my whole life, I need you now, I have you now. I will never let you go."

"I don't understand how you can be attracted to someone you can see right through. Whose every word is a rerun of shit you've already heard and seen in your mind's eye."

"Did you just say mind's eye, Deadëye?"

"Mindsæye."

"You just surprised me, Charles. I must be having a stroke."

"I want to see my fingers between your lips."

"Have I been drugged?"

"I don't drug people, why would I waste my drugs on people who may or may not appreciate them?"

"Date rape."

"Look, when a woman agrees to a date with Deadëye, she knows she's getting fucked. I have a form they sign. Any woman I have sex with had better be alert and constantly shifting gears. Creativity is very important to me."

"My sisters said something like that about you. You taught them so many new things."

"Everything I know, I learned from you."

"I didn't teach you felching."

"That's not entirely true. You thought about it…"

"THE CAUTIONARY TALE OF A ROCK 'N' ROLL BAND on drugs traveling the world eating acid and fucking your daughters, mother, sisters, and brothers is a bullshit trope," the ghost of Captain Kangaroo said. "Let the rock 'n' roll people do what rock 'n' roll people do—educate. Shut the fuck up and you might learn something. Listen, for once, and learn from the masters."

"Who the fuck is Captain Kangaroo?" Cambodian woman Sonya asked.

"Have you ever heard of Oprah," Deadëye asked the dumbass drummer.

"I've seen pictures. She looks like she belongs on some kind of food packaging."

"I think she's on beer bottles in Kazakstan. Anyway, that's not the point. If you keep fisting my wife, you're fired."

"When I stop fisting your wife you'd better take her to a bowling alley. Charlotte needs that shit balls deep. Literally," Sonya said. "You have insulted me and all of my ancestors. Give me a lot of money right now or you'll be wishing my auger was a fist."

"Your auger? Where the hell did you get an auger?"

"Same place I got the *Fantasy Animal Dildo Penis Sleeve Horse Cock Sheath Dog Knot Dick Extender Dragon Enlargement Adult Sex Toy*."

33
BARCELONA, BUSAN, BEYOND

Deadëye's search for a hotel in Barcelona revealed more than he expected. "Holy shit!"

"Now what?" Charlotte asked.

"We're not leaving Barcelona for three weeks, at least."

"Why is that, Mr. King?"

"Have you ever seen a human tower?"

"I've seen stacks of humans on the internet."

"Look what's happening in a couple of weeks." Deadëye showed Charlotte video clips from La Mercè, the biggest festival in Barcelona, including the death-defiers building human towers.

"Those people are insane!" Charlotte accurately diagnosed the human tower participants. "Is that a little kid or a little person climbing to the top of that thing?"

"Yes."

"I think we have found our people."

"Did you see this shit on the news?" Deadëye asked Charlotte.

"I'm sure I missed it."

"Homeless people are being given free hand grenades in Las Vegas."

"That sounds like a great idea, to me," Charlotte said. "Everybody in America has been at war with those people for years, maybe they can form some kind of homeless Hamas."

"That's an interesting take on the situation."

"It's bound to happen," Charlotte said. "Shouldn't we get a chance to watch that shit on TV before the planet is completely fucked? We're already seeing female CarJitsu."

"You make a good point. Do you have any rope?"

Charlotte's sisters hung around in Spain for a couple of days until the lure of Canadian food was too much for them to ignore anymore. Alone together in España, Mr. and Mrs. King shut themselves off from the rest of the world and lived their lives in the moment. For a week. Until the rock 'n' roll animals within awakened from their much-needed hibernation situation to feed voracious appetites for excessive volume and feedback. So Deadëye flew from

Barcelona to a city lacking anything of value in the world of rock 'n' roll—Seoul, South Korea.

South Korea is like a Japan without a personality or a soul. Two days of exploration revealed nothing of cultural value or interest, so the Kings rode the bullet train to Busan.

"Los Angeles has better Korean barbecue than Korea," Deadëye posited to his wife.

Charlotte brought up a topic Deadëye knew to avoid at any cost. "Why can't we ever find a Canadian restaurant anywhere?"

"Do you know why there are so many Thai restaurants every place in the world?" Deadëye asked Charlotte.

"So the Thai massage places will have a cover story for the hookers?"

"Yes," Deadëye answered, "and because the Thai government pays Thai people to open restaurants all over the world to promote Thai culture and tourism."

"That's smart," Charlotte said. "We need to open a Deadëye store in Seoul."

In the absence of 75% of her band, Maria found a Japanese Yngwie Malmsteen and recorded a thrash metal album with the cat/apple drummer. Doc went radio silent on his boat in America somewhere. Sonya may or may not have seduced the Dalai Lama and joined a harem.

Armed with comforting knowledge about the posse, Charlotte and Deadëye spent an uneventful evening in Busan then boarded a jet ferry to Japan.

"They call my wife the queen of rock 'n' roll; they call this boat the Ferrari of the seas," Deadëye told his wife.

"I don't care what they call me," Charlotte said. "I am Mrs. fucking King."

The race car-turned-boat dumped the Kings in Fukuoka. One evening there proved enough. Deadëye and Charlotte next rode the bullet train to Osaka with clear instructions to Doc that their availability in Tokyo hinged on Sonya's presence in Deadëye Studios Shinjuku. Seated at lunch in Osaka one day, Charlotte asked her husband, "Is that Hiro?"

Sure enough, the Hiro tour of Japan scouting Deadëye retail locations appeared beneath the second-floor terrace of the izakaya, prompting hilarity amongst the Kings.

"He's so fucking intense," Deadëye said.

Charlotte wondered, "Who are those dudes in suits he's barking at?"

Impressed by the assessed interest Hiro displayed on his critical mission with nobody watching, as far as he knew, the Kings relaxed and enjoyed the show as Hiro negotiated a lease for the most visible and prominent retail space in Osaka.

In Osaka, Charlotte unleashed her inner otaku while the power couple searched for the best takoyaki. Perhaps the most fun, to date, of the young couple's life together.

Under a full moon on a cloudless night, a bat signal in the sky above Osaka Bay told Deadëye and Charlotte the time had come—Tokyo beckoned. By midnight loud guitar amplifiers shook Shinjuku skyscrapers off of foundations as if Godzilla were walking down the street.

"Are we ready for this shit?" Deadeye asked his bandmates. Sonya's uncharacteristic silence concerned Charlotte.

"Are you okay, Sonya?" Charlotte asked the drummer.

Maria said, "Sonya took a vow of silence at the cult compound where they shaved her head."

"Awesome!" Deadeye screamed. "We don't have to listen to any of her bullshit!"

"Fuck you, Deadëye!" Sonya screamed, thus slamming a gavel down on a lectern ending the relative peace Deadëye had so cherished for 90 seconds.

The next morning Deadëye and Charlotte arrived in the studio, greeted by the sight of a rhythm section ready to rock and a team of Japanese dudes in lab coats.

"Who's sick?" Deadëye asked.

Maria said, "Hiro requires all of the studio personnel to wear lab coats."

"Fuck, yeah!" Deadëye said. "Hiro is becoming my new hero."

The band ran through every song they knew with tape machines running the entire time. After lunch, the band listened to the replay, loved what they heard, and instructed the rock 'n' roll doctors in the room to get that shit mastered and manufactured as soon as possible for a Japan-only, vinyl-only release. Deadëye handed the lab coat crew a shitload of yen from the Shinjuku safe with orders to get the vinyl pressed and packaged immediately. Charlotte's circus friend created the record's artwork.

By the time Doc appeared at Shinjuku HQ a week later, the studio and ground floor retail space overflowed with hundreds of boxes filled with two record sets pressed on 180-gram vinyl of the Deadëye band's christening of Deadëye Shinjuku.

"Holy fuck!" Doc said as he pulled a copy of the LP out of a box.

"Deadëye gets shit done," Sonya said.

"How's it sound?" Doc asked.

"Fuck you, Doc," Charlotte said. "We sound better than any band on the fucking planet. All day, every day, motherfucker."

"That's my wife," Deadëye said.

Hiro showed up not long after Doc and the Deadëye/Doc/Hiro brain trust decamped for an undisclosed location. With hookers. After that, they got down to business.

Deadëye said, "Hiro, we need our own stores all over the place. Stores where we can sell records, sell merch, host parties, play live shows, cut out the middleman—"

"We have 12 stores under construction in Japan. Also London, Stockholm, New York, Los Angeles, Nashville, New Orleans, and Montreal," Hiro said.

"Wow!" Doc exclaimed.

Hiro continued, "We don't pay any rent in Japan. My family owns buildings in every major city and a hundred other towns in Japan."

"What about Europe and North America?" Doc asked.

"Don't ask," Hiro said as he made the international sign language symbol for a yakuza missing a finger. "I'll just say, we're paying well-below-market rate rents everywhere outside of Japan."

Rusty wheels in Doc's head squealed back to life. "The U.S. tour starts in six weeks. New Orleans is the first city with a retail store on the tour. Then it's Los Angeles,

Montreal, and Nashville. Will those stores be ready for us to host grand opening parties while we're there?"

"New Orleans needs to go last—those fuckers are lazy there. Nothing happens fast in that town. Remember how long it took to send those people to send us water after the hurricane?" Who knew Hiro was trapped in the Superdome as a child after Hurricane Katrina?

"How are we filling all of the space in the stores? Records and T-shirts alone can't possibly fill all that space in Osaka," Deadëye said.

A shocked Hiro asked Deadëye, "How do you know about the space in Osaka?" triggering a sign language signal from Deadëye Hiro understood all too well.

Doc and Deadëye took a stroll around the back alleys of Shinjuku. "I ran over a water skier in Georgia," Doc reported. "The propeller chopped his head off."

"I'm sorry, Doc. What happened after that?"

"Good question," Doc answered. "I didn't stop to find out. From what I hear, the news reported the whole thing as a shark attack. I always tow a chum dispenser behind the boat in case I need sharks."

"People in Georgia are good for two things and I can never remember what the second one is."

"Hiro's about to make us a shitload of money," Doc said.

"Good," Deadëye responded. "Let's cut the U.S. tour down to a half-dozen shows and add a few more dates to Canada—Charlotte needs to be the Billie Whatshername of the Great White North."

"We can do that. As a matter of fact, we do this U.S. tour, and then, when we go back to America next year, we call that tour our U.S. farewell tour. America really sucks right now, Deadëye."

"So, we do a couple of store openings here, three weeks in America and Canada, then we're done for the rest of the year?"

"Yep," Doc answered. "Did you find a house for your wife?"

I think so," Deadëye answered. "The top two floors of a building in the Gràcia neighborhood of Barcelona. I'm calling the real estate guy and pulling the trigger right now."

"How tall's the building?"

"Six floors."

"As soon as the ink is dry on your deal for the top two floors, we buy the rest of the building. We meaning Hiro."

"That's a great idea."

The band spent three weeks in Japan rehearsing, recording, playing live shows, and hosting grand opening fiestas for Deadëye retail stores. Everything Deadëye touched turned to gold. Three weeks in Canada and America followed the same modus operandi, followed by an added week in Japan, then everybody took a break for two months. Mr. and Mrs. King hosted Charlotte's family in their Barcelona forever home for the holidays. Hiro popped in with his suit-wearing Japanese posse for an afternoon in early January to throw money around, purchasing the remainder of the units in the Kings' building plus the adjacent properties. Like a champion. Hiro and Deadëye pretended they didn't know each other so Hiro could look like the asshole when the neighborhood found out the entire block was owned by a foreigner. Shit happens.

Per a unanimous vote of the global Deadëye community, every Deadëye location featured a full-service bar, full-service restaurant, and entertainment establishments nine-fingered friends of the Deadëye business maintained at arm's length. Between the parking revenue and the hooker revenue, the Deadëye organization raked in so much cash it quietly became a major customer of the cash-counting machine business.

"We're getting rid of the cash-counting machines," Doc told Deadëye.

"Why?" Deadëye asked. "Is our business dying?"

"No," Doc answered, "not yet. We're switching to cash-weighing machines. Do you wanna hear what the plan for the year is?"

"Yes. please."

"Two weeks rehearsing and recording in West Hurley, three weeks in America, three weeks across Japan, New Zealand, and Australia. Six weeks of vacation, six weeks recording in your new studio in Barcelona, two months of European festivals in the summer, then four months off. Maybe an occasional, one-off show in Dubai or some shit like that, if the price is right."

"Sounds perfect."

"We all need time off to be normal, wealthy, people."

"Normal, wealthy, water skier-murdering, people."

"Now that you mention it, we do our best murdering on boats," Doc said.

"Motherfucker, Deadëye does its best murdering on stage," Deadëye clarified. "By the way, did we ever sell all of those Japanese LPs?"

"No, Hiro's sold a few hundred, but we've already made a fortune."

"How is that possible? We ordered 10,000!"

"Nobody can find the record anywhere. He sends one or two copies to each of the Deadëye stores a couple of times a month. People buy 'em and put 'em on eBay at insane prices. Hiro sells some on eBay at even more insane prices. It's a great fucking album and nobody can get their hands on it."

"That fucker's a genius. We need to take him to the Abba museum."

34 THE GHOST

"Doc, I need to lock myself in a room with an Olympic White Stratocaster and a Marshall stack for a week."

"Why?"

"The ghost of Jeff Beck came to me in a dream and told me my guitar playing is shit."

"Fuck!"

Doc knew, and he still knows, that when the ghost of Jeff Beck pays a visit and offers advice, you do what the ghost of Jeff fucking Beck says. Deadëye took over the Deadëye

Yokohama studio and studied under the tutelage of the ghost of Jeff Beck while Charlotte crafted a solo album later known to people in parts of Indonesia as the album that brought Charlotte to Bali on vacation that one time. After *Because, Charlotte* sold a gazillion copies worldwide. Deadëye's lifelong relationship with the ghost of Jeff Beck may or may not have been cut short by the yakuza or Doc's chum dispenser, nobody knows. Nothing lasts forever.

C HARLOTTE'S CONCERN WAS WRITTEN ALL OVER HER FACE. "Charles, tell me it's not true."

Oh no, she found out about the teenage maid cafe prodigy! "Do you want me to lie?"

Charlotte looked Deadeye squarely in his face and demanded, "Please! Tell me the aliens are not massing for an attack on our planet from bases on the other side of the moon!"

"Uh, okay. The aliens are not massing for an attack on our planet from bases on the other side of the moon," Deadëye said. "Everybody knows the moon is hollow and the aliens have bases inside the moon."

"I knew it! I can't trust you, Charles! Everybody knows the aliens are massing for an attack on our planet from their bases on the other side of the moon! Get out! We are finished! Our band is finished! Get out!"

Deadëye was devastated, depressed beyond belief, as he walked across the square to the hotel Hiro's multinational conglomerate owned. The Deadëye Suite, permanently reserved for such occasions, lacked for nothing except an ungrateful bitch, most would say.

"Doc, she's been brainwashed," Deadëye told his manager and trusted confidant. "She's like an even more scary Katy Perry."

"That means she's the hottest woman on the planet," Doc said. "Like a female Scary Gary."

"No," Deadëye said. "The hottest woman on the planet is the hottest woman who works for Hooters and stands next to the hottest weather woman on the Mexican television morning show."

"Are you talking about the show with the dude in the bumblebee costume?"

"I mean, if you're into that…"

"Do you know what fucking time it is in Mississippi?" Doc asked Deadëye.

"No," he answered. "My manager was smart enough to make sure my band never spent any time in Mississippi. Charlotte is done with me. Where do I find another Charlotte?"

"Do you want a list?" Doc asked. "Those bitches are a dime a dozen. You have no idea how hard me and Cam have worked to keep those whores away from you. Cam, especially."

"What? Why? I don't remember ever seeing shit like that in your job description."

"Whatever. You'll be fine. She'll be back, one day. In the meantime, you have carte blanche to visit places like Medellin and Bangkok where nobody knows who you are and every hot 18-year-old is a prostitute, by law."

"Don't you think it's a better idea to start in the Baltics? Maybe start in Estonia and work my way down from Tallinn to Vilnius?"

"Dude, you'll never make it to Vilnius. I can see you making it through Latvia, but there's no way you'll make it more than fifty kilometers into Lithuania before the wheels come off."

"Is that so bad?" Deadëye asked. "I quit. Find me a divorce lawyer. Fire the band. Close the stores. Sell all my shit. Shut it all down. I'll be in touch when I run out of cash."

"Where are you going? Really? It's fucking winter, nobody goes to Estonia in the winter."

"Is it winter in Malaysia?"

"No, but it's a holiday in Cambodia."

"I've heard that."

"Listen," Doc said, "you're not the only one with mixed emotions."

"What the fuck are you talking about? I don't have mixed emotions. Did you think I needed an emotional rescue or something?"

"Well, for a while you were walking around acting like you were some kind of a beast of burden."

"Did you hear that from the neighbors?"

"No, they said you were waiting on a friend."

"When I was walkin' after dark?"

"Is it any wonder?"

"Yes."

"Look, the smartest thing you can do right now is go to the airport, get on a plane, and fly to Miami. Right now. We'll cruise around on my boat, recharge the batteries, and find a way forward."

"Okay, motherfucker, I'll let you know when I'm in the air. We are the champions. We're going to DisneyWorld."

35
DEADËYE 2.0

Doc wasted no time at all ruining Deadëye's day. "Hiro isn't returning my calls. I'm told all the Deadëye stores were rebranded as Charlötte stores overnight."

"That bitch stole my umlaut?"

"Yeah, and most of your money, too."

"Fuck!"

"We're good, the stock market has worked in your favor like a motherfucker lately. And your rainy day fund is in the mid-eight figures. Charlotte is a young superstar of a woman who needs to be alone and be herself for a while.

She'll be back. And back and forth a few times. Up and down. Lettin' it all hang out. Shit like that. Use this time to do weird shit."

"Doc, fuck you. If you're gonna be a guru you need to look like Rick Rubin. Or Dr. Drew. You can't look like the hillbilly combination of the two with Down's Syndrome."

"That's not very nice. It's palsy."

"Her music sucks."

"Palsy, not Halsey. Anyway, we're hanging out with my friend, Paul Z, in Miami for a few days then we're going to Bermuda."

"I need a Pastram E sandwich."

"Anything else?"

"An ounce of cocaine, a case of tequila, and a couple of supermodel hookers, you moron! My wife just left me!"

"You'll need more supermodel hookers than that."

D EADËYE SANK INTO A DEEP, DARK, SUICIDAL DEPRESSION without Charlotte. Everyone in Deadëye's life turned out to be, decidedly, on Team Charlotte, except Doc. Doc, coincidentally, was the only one there from the very beginning—none of the other motherfuckers had a clue where their fame and fortune came from or how much work Deadëye and Doc put in before the gravy train hauling those ungrateful fucks left the station.

"Doc, we knew this would happen one day. We talked about it at length, in detail—it still sucks."

"When you're stuck in a rut, don't hang pictures," Doc said.

"What the fuck does that mean?"

"Don't dwell here, in misery, dumbass," Doc said. "Keep moving. Don't get stuck someplace you don't wanna be. Your career is on fire. You never needed that Canadian woman. She sure as fuck needed you."

"Fuck you, Doc. I know you're just trying to help, and I appreciate it. But I don't wanna hear any shit-talk about Charlotte. Get it?"

"Dude, she left you because you told her you don't believe aliens are massing on the dark side of the moon in preparation to invade Earth."

"You know this shit'll last a few weeks, right? My emotionally driven, irrational, stupid-as-fuck, intolerable insanity."

"I do. And I appreciate the way you pretend to be somewhat self-aware. I can't imagine the misery those cunts on Team Charlotte are experiencing."

"That bitch stole my umlaut."

"The predictable thing about animals is, they're unpredictable."

"Doc, you're the only friend I have left. And I know you have no other friends except for Paul Z. You know and I know that fucking drummer will be snorkeling her way here with a machete and a bad attitude any day now. I've got your back, in other words."

"Nice try. I don't need your help. I pity the fool who tries to snorkel up on me. Every shark on the East Coast is in my posse, Chum."

"Chüm…"

OVER BREAKFAST LOOKING OVER SHOULDERS the next morning Deadëye revealed his deepest, darkest dreams/nightmares.

"Doc, I wanna hit the road right now. In a convertible Cadillac with nothing but a guitar, a briefcase, and a toilet cam."

"Why don't you bring a 12-year-old Australian girl with you and call yourself ArmStröng?"

"Because I don't live in Silver Lake anymore, motherfucker."

"True or false: The three worst poser fake punk rock bands are Putrid, SoCal Distortion, and the Onspring."

"True. All of those bands totally suck. A lot of child molesters in those bands, too. A lot."

"I saw an article about suburban fans of suburban punk bands the other day. Ninety percent have been molested by a member of an emo band."

"Emo kids are the stupid kids."

"That's the thing. Emo bands run out of emo kids to molest before soundcheck, usually. So they molest every other kind of kid."

"Isn't Weezer credited with inventing emo?"

"Whoa! I never said that!"

"C'mon. Has any band ever looked more like the lineup on the Megan's Law website?"

"Do you think Zakk Wylde lives in the middle of nowhere because he can't live near a school?"

"Zakk Wylde is the dumbest motherfucker I have ever met, so I can't answer that question. It's probably because he's that rare combination of a total fucking moron and a kidfucker."

"Should he form a new band and call it Kidfücker?"

"Only if he can get the dude from ArmStrŏng in the band."

"Doc, what's your favorite album of all time?"

"I can't pick just one. It's a tie between *Born to Run* and *Fandango*."

"Jesus fucking Christ. That shit sucks. Do you have a gun on this boat? I need you to blow my head off."

"Yes. What's your favorite record?"

"*High as Hell*."

"That makes sense."

"You know Nashville Pussy?"

"A little bit. I worked with 'em for a few years. You need to put together a band like that. Nashville Pussy is a real band, not a pussy band like Deadëye."

Since Charlotte's lawyers found a way to freeze and seize all of their assets, Doc and Deadëye hit the road in Doc's mom's Astrovan and headed for shows booked in all of the Villes. Nashville, Jacksonville, Knoxville, Louisville…

"Why did we bring all of the guitars?" Deadëye asked Doc.

"We need to sell that shit so we can eat on the road. Not every venue has a catfish farm in the back of the juke joint on this tour."

"Do I have any friends left? There must be someone who isn't on Team Charlotte out of the thousands of people we've done business with."

"Nope," Doc answered. "Believe me, I've tried. Without hesitation, every single motherfucker we know is firmly rooted in the Team Charlotte camp."

"We're doomed."

"Totally," Doc agreed. "We're totally fucked. For now. Mark my words: cracks will appear in Charlotte's armor. You are her rock. Those who've forsaken you today will return. We understand, we are not resentful, we can't do a motherfucking thing about any of it right now. We do the same shit we've always done."

"What's that, again?"

"We push the button and take the ride."

"I think this part of the ride is gonna totally suck."

"You're overly optimistic. This will be the worst year of your fucking life. By far. However, there is a light at the end of the tunnel, you will make it out the other side of this."

"What's the point, then?"

"You're gathering material. Everybody hates the asshole whose life story is a nonstop happy dance. People wanna see a struggle, some tub-thumping."

"I don't even wanna—"

"You get knocked down, but you get up again, they're never gonna keep you down."

For some reason, those Chumbawamba lyrics cracked the shell Deadëye built around himself when Charlotte left. Doc made a grown man cry. Then Doc said, "I'll take you places that you've never, never seen."

And he did. Gainesville, Huntsville, Fayetteville, Greenville, Brownsville. Somewhere along the line, Doc found a T-shirt place to make DeadëyeVille merch. And he invited a music journalist from South America to join the traveling party and document Deadëye's rock bottom chapter. While Charlötte headlined stadiums and festivals

Deadëye dodged beer bottles in dive bars straddling the Mason-Dixon Line.

Deadëye never expected the South American dude's account of the tour to be read by anyone anywhere. So he was a brick house, lettin' it all hang out. Boy, was he wrong. *Washed-up Rocker Washes Up in Petrol Station* and *Deadëye Nearly Dead* were Doc's favorite headlines. A popular quote of Deadëye's in the Argentine media turned out to be, "I've played some shitholes before, but College Station, Texas takes the cake. If there's a college in this town you could've fooled me. If a husband and wife in College Station get a divorce, are they still brother and sister?"

The Astrovan needed far more refueling than any other Astrovan, according to Deadëye's quick math. Apparently, Doc was developing an addiction to tabloid journalism.

Doc did everything he could to shield Deadëye from his ex-wife's ubiquitous media presence. He was very successful, in fact, until Doc stopped for gas at a QuickTrip in West Virginia equipped with television screens in the gas pumps.

"Charlötte King Superstar?" Deadëye screamed. "The bitch stole my umlaut, my last name, and now she's fuckin' Jesus?"

Sure enough, Charlötte King's World Superstar Tour was a big deal in big cities while DeadëyeVille shows often served as opportunities for Southern Ohio bars to shut down early on weeknights.

Doc tried everything to help Deadëye shift his focus away from his suicidal depression.

"Doc, you know I hate golf."

Doc stared at Deadëye and said, "This isn't golf, you dumbfuck. This is Top Golf, the world's greatest golf superstore theme park for weird old cunts."

"That explains a lot," Deadëye said. "Anyway, what's our plan here? I don't wanna wait around for 20 years like that guy in Styx did for their reunion tour."

"You're good," Doc said. "You can do the Steve Perry thing and let a karaoke singer from Manila do all the touring while you cash the checks."

"How much money does that guy need to make to be considered wealthy in the Philippines?"

"How much money does a Happy Meal cost?"

"Where have all the good times gone?"

"Remember walking in the sand?"

"Remember walking hand-in-hand?"

"Doc, we've been to the edge."

"We stood and looked down."

"We lost a lot of friends there."

"Gamblin's for fools."

"That's the way I like it."

"I don't wanna live forever."

"I've got two tickets to paradise."

"I'll pack my bags. Can we leave tonight?"

"I woke up this morning and I got myself a beer."

"Is our future uncertain?"

"Yes. And the end is always near."

"Are we out of drugs, Doc."

"I'm afraid so, Deadëye, I'm afraid so."

"This drug problem in America is out of control."

"Stay calm. Don't be alarmed."

"Don't be alarmed? Stay calm? We're back at the funny farm if we're out of fucking drugs!"

"Maybe we need a few days without drugs," Doc said.

"And maybe you need an axe wound in the back of your head! You have one job, Doc. Maintain the inventory. You are the postmaster, I am the envelope. No matter what happens, the envelope gets a fucking stamp. When the fucking postmaster runs out of stamps, the entire operation no longer exists. It's kaput. You're not gonna let that happen in Deadëye's ZIP code, are you?"

"Well, sometimes—"

"Hey. Doc, I know you mean well, and we've been through our ups and downs. You deserve all the credit for our success."

"Thanks, Deadëye."

"Don't thank me yet. Thank me when you're on a fucking tugboat eating mosquitos out of your beard in St. Louis. You had one job. You failed. The little drug pocket in my jeans is empty. You're fired."

"Deadëye, I just want you to know, my own personal drug pocket has been empty for two weeks. Throughout our drug famine, I have forsaken drugs and suffered, personally, in order to provide you with that which humans require to navigate this 21st-century hellscape."

"Please, no need to be so dramatic. Anyway, get the fuck out of here. If I let you run out of drugs and I don't fire your fucking ass, it sets a bad precedent."

"I understand, Deadëye. I want you to know, like Whitney said, I will always love you."

"Sing it or you don't really mean it."

The new, improved, Deadëye hit the road solo-style and Howlin' Wolf style in a Pontiac station wagon with one Olympic white Stratocaster and the one Fender tweed combo amp on the planet Joe Bonamassa didn't have stashed in that shithole of a neighborhood prone to fires, floods, earthquakes, and serial killers. Don't believe the hype—Laurel Canyon is a shithole. The cartel's minimum purchase was $600 and nobody would deliver a pizza to Deadëye's place during the pandemic, so he got the fuck out of there. Allegedly.

With nothing but a mobile phone and a burnt orange vehicle for a home, Deadëye's lonely roadshow landed in Athens, Georgia with a Taco Tuesday thud. A confused and unprepared audience numbering in the high single digits and aged near triple digits witnessed history that night before the bingo started. Talladega, Tuscaloosa, Tupelo, Texarkana, and Shreveport rounded out the shitty South before Deadëye embarked on a mission to conquer Texas. For no particular reason. Towns and cities with the weirdest names (Waxahachie, Flower Mound, Pflugerville) topped the list of places most appealing to Deadëye, as did those with large prisons, which was pretty much every place in Texas. Deadëye sold enough T-shirts, records, and CDs to pay for gas, barbecue, beer, and truck stop speed along the highways and byways of Texas. For the children.

O THER THAN RANDOM STRIPPERS, BARTENDERS, Waffle House waitresses, Walmart cashiers, and down-and-out banjo players, Deadëye had nobody to talk to anymore

—the entire world he had once inhabited no longer existed. The hour or so he spent on a folding chair in the middle of a dilapidated bowling alley lounge was his sustenance, so Deadëye refused to believe his eyes when Hiro appeared in the sparse crowd at a New Braunfels barbecue joint.

Hiro didn't even say hello. "Let's go, this is fucking sad," Hiro said as he and Deadëye abandoned the Deadëye Wagon, drove to Austin, and boarded a plane bound for Tokyo.

"We can rebuild you," Hiro said. "Japanese people only know the old Deadëye."

"What am I going to do in Japan?" Deadëye asked Hiro.

"We need a manager for the Charlötte store in Yokohama."

"Sounds good to me," Deadëye said. "What I really wanna do is find a drummer and a bass player and do a power trio."

"I know," Hiro said. "I have a band waiting for you in Tokyo. And I kept a secret safe full of yen nobody knows about. I knew those fuckers would fuck you one day."

"Honestly, I think I'm the one who fucked it all up," Deadëye said. "Everything got so complicated…"

"In Japan, nobody knows. Nobody cares. Japan needs loud rock 'n' roll and Japanese people can't do what you do."

"That's racist, Hiro."

"Suck my dick, Niig—"

"Dude, don't even think about using that word."

"I was about to say, Niigata is the first stop on the Japan tour."

"Are there any drugs in that secret safe?"

"Yes. Doc's dead."

"What? How? When? Fuck!"

"He pissed off a pod of orcas and they capsized his boat. There wasn't much left."

"Killer whales ate Doc?"

"In Japan, we call that reverse sashimi."

"In America, we call that SeaWorld. What were Doc's last words before he went boating that day?"

"I don't know."

"You feed the dogs, I'll feed the fish."

"Orcas are mammals," Hiro said.

"Kangaroos have pockets. And kangaroos can't swim."

"Yes, they can. They go surfing, too."

"Is there anything else I need to know?"

"Your wife's in prison."

"Where?"

"Guatemala."

"Thanks for the update."

"I got you a job hosting the Japanese version of *Wheel of Fortune*."

"How the hell does that work? Isn't each character an entire word?"

"Sometimes. It makes the game much more difficult."

"Do Japanese people have spelling bees?"

"No. Japanese people all know how to spell words. We have schools in Japan." Twenty-nine hours after Hiro walked into the Texas barbecue joint and saved Deadëye from a lifetime of liver damage, the pair of maniacs landed in Tokyo. After clearing customs, Deadëye and Hiro emerged from the airport prison system where a woman with dead eyes in a chauffeur's costume awaited their arrival holding a "Deadeyes" sign above her head.

"You motherfucker," Deadëye said to Hiro as he watched his traveling companion laugh his ass off. The most beautiful woman in the world failed to maintain her blasé, limousine driver persona as Deadëye and Charlotte collapsed into each other in a heap of mixed emotions. Outside the terminal, Mr. and Mrs. King boarded the first hotel shuttle van they saw and gave Hiro the finger as their ride departed for a mystery accommodation location.

Plans for the future, accounts of the past, business matters, music, and mutual acquaintances didn't come up in any of their conversations during the time Deadëye and Charlotte spent together at the runway-adjacent hotel in Narita—the Kings lived in the moment as never before for a couple of days.

"Where do we go from here?" Deadëye asked Charlotte one day.

"I don't care where I go as long as it's with you," Charlotte replied. "Let's go somewhere new. Surprise me."

And that's how Charlotte and Deadëye wound up in Macau.

"You like places where dissimilar cultures collide," Charlotte said as the Kings strolled through the Las Vegas of a former Portuguese colony in China-ish.

"I also like places where I can watch kangaroos swimming."

"That sounds almost as entertaining as the Puppy Bowl," Charlotte said.

"Ya know, there's a reason you're the only one for me, Charlotte. There's nothing like the Puppy Bowl, and there's no one like you."

"That's what the Scorpions said. And women like me don't grow on trees."

"You are correct. Women like you don't grow on trees," Charles told his wife. "Did you know, there are tree kangaroos?"

"Did you know, you'll never, ever, find another woman you can have this conversation with?"

"Did you know, I wouldn't want to have this conversation with any another woman?"

"Yes, you would. We're finding an acrobat somewhere around here tonight."

"Tree kangaroos are acrobats."

FINIS.

ABOUT BLACK PATRICK

A resident of Los Angeles, California, Black Patrick dreams of the day everything he does is made possible by a generous grant from The Ralph M. Parsons Foundation.

Black Patrick is known to Americans as a single, successful man, unafraid of most things except heights, giant hornets, and people who believe it's a good idea to give birth to other people.

Black Patrick enjoys long walks on the beach, loud guitars, and handjobs in movie theaters. In his spare time, Black Patrick memorizes the encyclopedia. Banned from most bars in his adopted hometown of Los Angeles, Black Patrick spends a shitload of time writing fictional accounts of real people doing incredible things in unbelievable ways. And thinking about Gwendy doing incredible things in unbelievable ways. On Mexican television. With the guy in the bumblebee costume. On all fours. Again.

More than anything, Black Patrick is a refinery. A filter. The man who eliminates the bullshit and delivers the goods. Black Patrick appreciates your willingness and ability to read whatever amalgamation of honesty, reality, depravity, and fantasy the hadron collider in his head feeds the computer on his desk. With your help, Black Patrick will one day realize his ultimate dream and open that bowling alley in Vilnius.

How does Black Patrick do so much with so little? Narcotics help. And Black Patrick puts in the fuckin' work. He pours his entire, lived, existence into every sentence, every page, every chapter. You know what I'm talkin' about.

Some say, "Despite heavy drug and alcohol use, Black Patrick maintains a clarity of vision unseen in romance novel circles since the death of Edgar Allen Poe." People say a lot of things. Rest assured, when Black Patrick delivers his version of an idealized human existence to you, the reader, the student, the incarcerated, perhaps, it is with the expectation its content and its presentation is worth your time. Every. Fucking. Time.

People once thought people who thought flying airplanes on and off of boats were crazy and it would never happen. Those people suffered from a lack of motherfucking imagination. They were probably illiterate cunts proud of being born and raised somewhere they were even more proud of living their entire lives. What kind of incurious motherfucker lives their entire life in one place? A motherfucking cunt, that's who. Avoid that person like Black Patrick avoids losers who believe women named Thuy are capable of doing more than one thing with that hole in a face.

Black Patrick's remarkable, eleven-decade career in the entertainment industry and as a licensed examiner of many things has established him as one of the most powerful adult film stars alive today.

MORE FROM
BLACK PATRICK

A CHAMPION IN ACTION
WHO KNEW BLACK PATRICK COULD DELIVER SUCH A POWERFUL ROMANCE NOVEL? WHERE DID BLACK PATRICK FIND THE REMARKABLE COURAGE TO EXPOSE HIMSELF IN SUCH A PROFOUND WAY? WHAT FORCE OF NATURE PIERCED THE IMPENETRABLE COAT OF ARMOR SUFFOCATING BLACK PATRICK? DID BLACK PATRICK FINALLY DISCOVER A SIDE OF HIMSELF VISIBLE TO ALL BUT HIMSELF?

THE LAST RESORT
A MAN WALKS INTO A BAR. THE BARTENDER SAYS, "HEY, WE HAVE A DRINK NAMED AFTER YOU!" IF YOU ARE THAT MAN WALKING INTO THE BAR, TURN AROUND AND GET THE HELL OUT OF THERE. RUN. YOU ARE ABOUT TO GET DRUGGED, ROBBED, RAPED, AND MURDERED. IN THAT ORDER, ON A TUESDAY.

THE CONFIDENT MAN
WHO CAN SAY NO TO THAT FACE? THE MOTHERFUCKER CAN SELL ICE CUBES TO PENGUINS, WATER TO DOGS, AND YOUR SOUL FOR MORE THAN A DOLLAR AT THE DOLLAR STORE. HE'S PLAYING POKER WITH YOUR DOG RIGHT NOW.

A TASTE OF SOMETHING ELSE
FASTEN A BELT OF SOME KIND AND LEARN WHAT IT'S LIKE TO EAT, DRINK, BREATHE, AND SNORT ROCK 'N' ROLL. OR ELSE THE TERRORISTS HAVE WON. FOR THE CHILDREN.

BPP
BLACK PATRICK
PUBLISHING

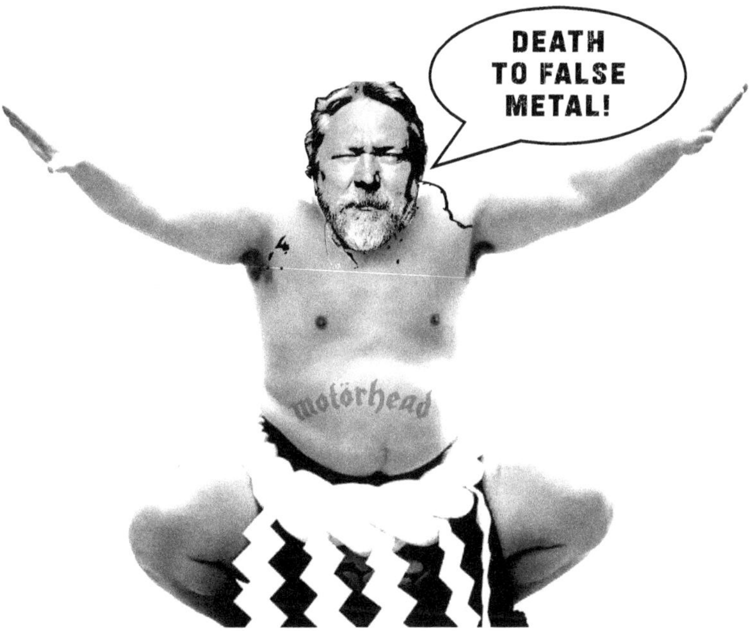
DEATH
TO FALSE
METAL!
motörhead